A night before camp disaster

Ma was sewing one last name tape onto a pair of green camp shorts. "Calm *down*, honey," she said. "You look like you're going to jump out of your skin."

"I can't help it." Abby distractedly crammed the T-shirt into her overstuffed suitcase. "I've waited so long and now it's almost here—my super-fantabulous, perfectly perfect summer."

Right before dinner, the phone rang.

"It's me." Merle's voice had a funny echo.

"I *know* that," Abby said. "Where have you been?"

Merle sounded like she was taking a deep breath. "You're not going to believe this," she said quickly, "but I'm at Lenox Hill Hospital. During dance class, I fell and broke my ankle."

"BROKE YOUR ANKLE?" Abby stared into the phone.

"I'm going to be in a cast for at least *four* weeks."

"FOUR WEEKS! You poor kid." That was a shocker! But there was a bright side. "Hey, now you won't have to worry about any of the sports stuff at camp!"

There was an uneasy pause. "Abby, don't you see? . . . I can't go."

Yours Till Niagara Falls, Abby

by JANE O'CONNOR

illustrated by Margot Apple

PUFFIN BOOKS

PUFFIN BOOKS
Published by the Penguin Group
Penguin Young Readers Group, 345 Hudson Street, New York, New York 10014, U.S.A.
Penguin Group (Canada), 90 Eglinton Avenue East, Suite 700, Toronto, Ontario, Canada M4P 2Y3
(a division of Pearson Penguin Canada Inc.)
Penguin Books Ltd, 80 Strand, London WC2R 0RL, England
Penguin Ireland, 25 St Stephen's Green, Dublin 2, Ireland (a division of Penguin Books Ltd)
Penguin Group (Australia), 250 Camberwell Road, Camberwell, Victoria 3124, Australia
(a division of Pearson Australia Group Pty Ltd)
Penguin Books India Pvt Ltd, 11 Community Centre, Panchsheel Park, New Delhi - 110 017, India
Penguin Group (NZ), 67 Apollo Drive, Rosedale, North Shore 0632, New Zealand
(a division of Pearson New Zealand Ltd)
Penguin Books (South Africa) (Pty) Ltd, 24 Sturdee Avenue, Rosebank, Johannesburg 2196, South Africa

Registered Offices: Penguin Books Ltd, 80 Strand, London WC2R 0RL, England

First published in the United States of America by Hastings House, Publishers, Inc., 1979
Published by PaperStar, a member of The Putnam Berkley Group, Inc., 1997
This edition published by Puffin Books, a division of Penguin Young Readers Group, 2008

1 3 5 7 9 10 8 6 4 2

THE LIBRARY OF CONGRESS HAS CATALOGED THE HASTINGS HOUSE EDITION AS FOLLOWS:
O'Connor, Jane.
Yours till Niagara falls, Abby.
SUMMARY: Abby faces two months of summer camp without her best friend.
[1. Camping—fiction. 2. Friendship—fiction]
I. Apple, Margot. II. Title
PZ7.0222YO [Fic] 79-19782

Puffin Books ISBN 978-0-14-241151-3

For my mother and father

1

NEVER IN ALL her life had Abby Kimmel been so filled with a sense of purpose. Her best friend was in trouble and she was coming to the rescue. It was that simple . . . or almost.

It had started yesterday. After school Abby raced over to Merle's apartment. *Blood of the Vampire* was on the 4:30 movie and they'd both looked forward to watching it all week.

The Diamonds lived on the top floor of an old New York City brownstone and Abby never liked standing alone in the dark, creepy hallway. She pressed hard on the doorbell.

There were footsteps inside and in a second Merle's mother opened the door looking flustered. "Abby! *Sweety*. Am I glad to see you." Mrs. Diamond was puffing away on an unlit cigarette. "I'm *frantic*. Honestly, the way Merle's carrying on! But she'll listen to you. . . . She'd go to the *moon* if you told her to."

Abby rushed in to find Merle sprawled face down on her bed, crying with abandon. "Merle? What's the matter?" She had never seen Merle so upset. Usually she was so calm and unexcitable. It was Abby who was always facing one crisis after another.

"Oh, Abby I can't believe they're doing this." Merle

sat up and hiccuped loudly. "They're sending me away this summer—to *camp!*"

"Wow, you at camp!" Abby exclaimed. "No offense—I'm not exactly Tracy Austin myself—but you're *hopeless* at sports."

"I know, I know," Merle said miserably, hiccuping again. "Only Dad's going to be in summer stock on Cape Cod—"

"So? Can't you just go, too? You got to go to Disneyworld when he did that TV special." Abby thought Merle was incredibly lucky to have an actor for a father. She got to go to so many neat places. Abby's father was just a tax lawyer and the one time she'd been taken along on a business trip she'd eaten a rotten eclair and thrown up for two days.

"I'd love to go to Cape Cod," Merle sniffed. "Only Mom has got it into her head that I'm going to turn out warped or something from spending so much time around actors. She wants me to have a normal summer outdoors with kids my own age. She says I'll be *enriched* by the experience."

Abby groaned in sympathy. "She makes you sound like a slice of Wonderbread, for God's sake!"

"You've just got to think of some way to get me out of this." Merle reached over to her night table and handed Abby a brochure for Camp Pinecrest. The soggy, tear-stained pages were checkered with photographs of girls playing softball, playing basketball, playing hockey. There were girls sitting cross-legged around a campfire, girls weaving rather lopsided-looking baskets and girls waterskiing while they waved enthusiastically at the camera. And every single one of them was grinning from ear to ear. Just looking at all those smiles almost made Abby's jaws ache. But the girls sure looked like they were having fun.

Abby stared at those smiles for a minute. "I hate to tell you," she said, "but I honestly think this place looks kind of nice. The kids in the pictures don't exactly look like they're suffering."

Merle snorted contemptuously. "That's easy for you to say."

"No, Merle. I mean it," Abby said thoughtfully. "After all, camp can't be *just* sports. Look here," she pointed at the brochure. "I bet you get to sleep in little tents and tell ghost stories and roast marshmallows." Abby plopped down on the bed and leaned against the wall. "I bet it's more fun than staying in some rented house at some dumb beach every summer. All I do is get sunburned and listen to Ma yelling that I shouldn't swim out past my *ankles*. And there are never any kids around. Just Emily."

Now it was Merle's turn to groan sympathetically. Merle disliked Abby's sister Emily, who was four and a half and horrible, almost as much as Abby did.

Suddenly Abby sat bolt upright. "Hey, wait a minute!" She clutched the brochure tightly and the look in her eyes became feverish. "What if we could go to camp *together* . . ."

"Together!" Merle sat up. "Oh, Abby! If you were with me, it would be okay."

"Okay!" Abby said. "I think it'd be great—like one long sleepover!" And it struck Abby that all her truly spectacular ideas seemed to come to her this way. In a flash. "Now shhh. I want to read this brochure more carefully." Abby cleared her throat. " *'Camp Pinecrest, pearl of Lake Pocahontas,'* " she read aloud. " *'Are you a happy, healthy, fun-loving girl between the ages of eight and fourteen?'* Yes, of course. *'Are you looking for eight weeks of unforgettable fun?'* " She looked at Merle and shrugged her shoulders. "Sure, why not? *'Are you ready to explore new horizons?'* "

"No!" said Merle emphatically. "That sounds scary."

Abby rolled her eyes. "Don't be such a poop." But actually that question had stopped her too. She liked to think of herself as adventurous. And to the outside world Abby knew she appeared bold and confident—"spunky" was what Grandma called her—because she wisecracked so much. But down deep Abby wondered whether she was brave at all or just had a big mouth. After all what "exploring" had she done? She'd gone to the same school since kindergarten, lived in the same apartment all her life, known all the same kids for as long as she could remember. And she was happy that way. She liked counting on things to stay exactly as they'd always been. Like her friendship with Merle. That was one thing that would never change, for sure. Abby smiled at her friend. "Merle, don't worry about that part. Look, I'd be petrified too if I had to go alone, not knowing anybody. But if we both went, then that wouldn't be a problem."

Merle seemed to see the logic in that. "But do you think they'd ever say yes? Your parents, I mean."

Abby pushed away Merle's worry with a careless wave of her hand. "Of course they'll say yes. They'll think it's a terrific idea. Ma especially. She's always saying how she'd love to see what I'd do without her around to pick up after me and keep track of all the stuff I forget." Abby jumped off the bed. "Listen. Just leave everything to me. I'll talk to Ma and Daddy tonight and I'll write for more brochures."

Merle managed a grateful watery smile. "Abby, I knew you'd come through for me. What would I ever do without you?"

Abby socked her in the arm affectionately. "If you can't count on your best friend, who can you count on?"

"I feel better already," Merle was saying as she led Abby to the front door. "Listen, I'll come over tomorrow right after my dance lesson. The original *Dracula* is on 'Monster Matinee.' "

"Vonderful," Abby crooned, imitating her idol, Bela Lugosi. "Duhn't be late." She rolled her eyes and swooped out the door. "I vill be vaiting."

2

THE KIMMELS' apartment was on the fourth floor of a big, red brick building overlooking Central Park. With a sinking feeling in her stomach, Abby looked out the living room window and watched Merle, punctual as always, hurrying up the block. Abby had the front door open by the time Merle got off the elevator.

Immediately Merle pounced on her. "What'd they say?" she shouted, practically shaking Abby.

"They said no," Abby admitted lamely.

"Doomed! I'm doomed," Merle wailed while she hung up her parka. That was Merle: even in times of stress, she was neat.

"Now don't get upset. I'm not giving up." Abby swung a protective arm around Merle's shoulders. "Nobody nudges like I nudge. So just give me time. Ma and Daddy will come around." She steered Merle into her room and put up the Do Not Disturb sign which, unfortunately, had never yet kept Emily from barging in.

"So give me the gory details," Merle said, slumping in Abby's rocker.

"Well," Abby sighed, "first Ma said she was very sorry you were unhappy about camp but that was no reason for me to go—just to cheer you up." She paused. "But if you ask me, the big problem is they don't take me seriously. Daddy kept bringing up all my other ideas that didn't turn out like I thought. Like the trumpet lessons.''

"No offense but that's true.''

Abby frowned. Merle had the irritating habit of being totally objective. "How was I to know you needed lungs like King Kong to play that instrument?''

"Yeah but you quit Brownie troop, too, right away.'' Merle pointed out, rocking maddeningly back and forth in the squeaky rocker. "And remember last spring when you got me to chip in on those lemons with you? We only had our lemonade stand two days before you decided it was boring. We lost a fortune! And—''

"Okay, okay,'' Abby broke in impatiently. She turned up the TV volume. "Whose side are you on anyway?''

Abby scowled at the television screen. Of course it was true some of her ideas hadn't been perfect. But if a plan didn't work out like you expected, why bother to stick it out? That wasn't being a quitter, like Merle and Daddy made it seem. That was just being smart. "Anyway,'' Abby said defensively, "going to camp together is different. It really *is* a great idea. I just have to convince Ma and Daddy.''

Then she shut up. A ghostly apparition floated across the screen followed by a blood-curdling scream. "Monster Matinee'' was starting.

In answer to Abby's special delivery letter, an envelope from Camp Pinecrest arrived the next Monday and Abby immediately went to work scattering brochures in strategic places—under her parents' pillows, on the mail table in the front hall, even inside the refrigerator.

"You should see," Abby whispered to Merle during study hall. "I practically wallpapered the apartment with those brochures. And I'm gonna leave little poems for them to find. Here's one I just thought up. . . . 'Be a buddy, Be a champ. Send Abby Kimmel to Pinecrest Camp.'—Not bad, huh?"

"I pray it works," Merle whispered from behind her math book.

"It'll work," Abby assured her and then began doodling in her notebook so the study hall monitor would think she was studying.

That night after dinner Ma fished into her knitting bag and came up with a brochure instead of the mittens she was making for Emily. "Now honey, I thought we'd been through all this," Ma said to Abby. "And stop smiling at me that way—I'm not as big a pushover as you think."

Abby draped herself over the back of her mother's chair and said sweetly, "But I'm just trying to prove this isn't a whim—that I'm really serious about camp, that I'm—"

"An impossible itch," Daddy said, coming into the living room and giving Abby a friendly swat on the rear. "Now drop it, Ab. The case is closed."

Her parents weren't budging. Not an inch. For two weeks Abby tried reasoning; she tried pleading; and then she tried whining even though she knew that was a big mistake. *"Everybody* my age goes to sleepaway camp.

It'll be the Hartman twins' third year at tennis camp."
But her arguments fell on deaf ears.

Merle was growing morbidly philosophical about the situation. "After all, what's *one* miserable summer?" she said as they slogged through the snow one morning on their way to school. "Mom says I'm too dependent on you anyway and that it'll be better for me to be on my own."

Abby stopped right in her tracks. "That's ridiculous," she protested. "We depend on each other." She clasped Merle's wet, snowy mitten in her bare hand and they continued walking. "Only I let you down when I kept saying I wouldn't. I feel awful." Abby was all set to launch into a long attack on parents in particular and the unfairness of life in general when she glanced at the bank clock on Broadway. "Eight-fourteen!" she gasped and they both ran the last two blocks, raced up school steps, and collapsed in their seats just ahead of the late bell.

3

IT WAS ALMOST midnight. Abby had sneaked into the kitchen where she quietly dialed Merle's number. She prayed Merle's parents wouldn't pick up and they didn't. "Hey, it's me," Abby whispered into the receiver. "Have I got *great* news!"

"I could use some. Dad sent in the check for camp."

"Cheer up." Abby glanced down the hall to make sure her parents weren't coming. "I overheard Ma and Daddy talking tonight and guess what? They're coming around. They were saying how maybe camp isn't such a bad idea after all."

"No kidding! Do you really think there's a prayer—"

"I just know everything's going to turn out exactly like we planned," Abby crowed into the phone. "But it's weird. It's like those Chinese handcuffs I have. The harder I tried with Ma and Daddy, the less I got anywhere. Now when I give up, suddenly things go my way. OOPS! I hear Ma. Gotta go!"

Abby's parents sprang the good news—a surprise, they thought—during Saturday morning breakfast.

"You won't ever regret this decision," Abby said hugging them both.

"I should hope not," Daddy grumbled good-naturedly, "for what it's costing."

In celebration Abby and Merle had lunch at Mel's Pizza, then saw two Boris Karloff movies.

"Can you believe it?" Abby remarked once again when they emerged from the theater, blinking at the daylight. "Can you *really* believe how everything turned out so perfectly?"

"Yeah," said Merle. "It was neat the way they got the mad scientist in the end."

"Dodo, I mean about camp. A whole summer together!"

"Yeah, that part is neat. Only I still can't get worked up about playing softball for eight weeks."

"How many times do I have to tell you?" Abby said impatiently. "It's not going to be that way—you'll see when the camp director comes."

Matilda Terwilliger or Aunt Tillie, as she said all the campers called her, arrived at the Kimmels' on a Saturday afternoon. Everyone—Merle and her parents, Ma and Daddy, even Emily—was on hand to greet her. Loaded down with a slide projector and slides, Aunt Tillie marched into the living room. She was very short and plump with cottony white hair, but jolly was not a word Abby would have picked to describe her. There was something about Aunt Tillie that made Abby feel as though she'd better sit up straight and behave. And she had a sharp way of speaking, as if she were snipping off the end of each sentence with a scissors.

"She looks mean," Emily announced in a stage whisper.

Abby poked her sister and covered up with a smile as introductions were being made.

"So. Here are the two girls. Who is who?" Aunt Tillie asked in imperious tones.

"That's Merle," offered Mrs. Diamond. Merle seemed to shrink behind her mother.

"Don't be bashful, Merle. You must learn to speak up." Aunt Tillie switched her penetrating gaze. "And this must be Abigail."

"Only everybody calls me Abby." Abby hoped she didn't sound as timid as she felt.

"You are the girl who wrote me—I like a girl with initiative!" Aunt Tillie followed that pronouncement by removing all the pictures on one wall of the living room. "Now, let's get down to business, shall we?" She bustled about, moving chairs, setting up her projector, shooing off all efforts of Daddy and Mr. Diamond to help.

Merle rolled her eyes at Abby, which made her feel uneasy. She burrowed deeper into her armchair. This wasn't how she had pictured Aunt Tillie at all. She seemed too much like a principal. But of course! Abby smiled to herself. Now she understood. Aunt Tillie was probably like all those old pioneer women in westerns—gruff on the outside but underneath very kind and lovable.

With this consoling picture, Abby settled back to watch the slides that flashed on the living room wall while Aunt Tillie described a typical day at Pinecrest. "A bugle awakens the whole camp at 7:00," Aunt Tillie began, "and by 7:20 everybody is at the flagpole field for 'The Pledge of Allegiance.' " As Aunt Tillie ran through the schedule, it seemed to Abby as if they'd need about fifty hours in a day to pack in all the activities. Why there was one sport—something called newcombe—that she'd never even heard of! Abby stole a sideways glance at Merle who looked positively ashen. Everyone else, however, seemed impressed.

"Ooh, Bambi!" Emily squealed over a slide of a deer while all the parents kept oohing and ahhing over the beautiful scenery.

"It does look gorgeous," Abby whispered encouragingly to Merle. "With the lake and all those pine trees."

"They don't have tents like you said," Merle whispered back.

"I think the cabins look nice. They're probably more comfortable than tents anyway." She wished Merle would stop being so negative.

Mrs. Diamond beamed at every mention of "healthy outdoor life" and Ma nodded enthusiastically when Aunt Tillie mentioned "instilling a sense of responsibility in each girl."

"To me camp is first and foremost a learning experience," Aunt Tillie said with an emphatic finger pointed at her audience. Abby avoided Merle's eyes. "Eight weeks at Pinecrest can't fail to change a girl."

Abby did not like the sound of those words. But then it suddenly hit her why Aunt Tillie was acting this way. Abby almost laughed out loud. Boy was she dumb for not figuring it out sooner!

As soon as Aunt Tillie left with a firm handshake for everybody and a promise to see the girls on June 28th, Merle beat a hasty retreat to Abby's room and flopped on her bed. "Talk about strict! I knew it was going to be like that. I just knew it. Only half an hour free period a day. In bed by 8:30. Brother!''

Abby sat down in her rocker and tried to reason with Merle. "Relax. You're getting all worked up over nothing.''

"I won't last a week at that place,'' Merle insisted.

"Look, Merle, I admit I was getting a little nervous, too, until I figured out what was going on.'' Abby leaned forward in her rocker. "Don't you see? She *has* to make it sound that way. You saw how my mother was falling for it. Yours too. If Aunt Tillie made camp sound like too much fun, I bet nobody would send their kids there.''

Merle hesitated. "Do you really think that's it?''

"I'm sure. Listen, you read the brochures too. Didn't they make the place sound like fun?'' Merle gave a small nod. "Well? So stop worrying. The brochures can't lie. Otherwise, Aunt Tillie could be sued for false advertising!''

"Gee, I hadn't thought of it like that,'' Merle said.

Abby smiled. She could always get Merle to see things her way. "Just think how terrific it will be. The whole summer together. No parents around to bug us. No Emily!''

"You're right, Ab,'' Merle said. "It's going to be great.'' And Abby noted with satisfaction that *finally* Merle sounded enthusiastic.

"If only it weren't so far off.'' Abby turned to the "Great Moments from the Movies'' calendar above her head. "We've got all of April and May and practically all of June to get through." She fished in one of her desk drawers and pulled out a red marker. "Well, we might as well start our countdown now," she said and ceremoniously made a nice, neat X through the date.

Each morning after that, as soon as she got up, Abby made sure to cross out one more box on her calendar. Time seemed to creep by with maddening slowness. But soon Abby had a whole week of X's, and eventually a month's worth, and finally, FINALLY, all the days had X's through them. It was June 27th. She and Merle were actually leaving for camp the next day.

Abby was beside herself with excitement. She couldn't even concentrate on packing. She kept folding and refolding the same Pinecrest T-shirt over and over again.

Ma was sewing one last name tape onto a pair of green camp shorts. "Calm *down*, honey," she said. "You look like you're going to jump out of your skin."

"I can't help it." Abby distractedly crammed the T-shirt into her overstuffed suitcase. "I've waited so long and now it's almost here—my super-fantabulous, perfectly perfect summer."

Ma put a gentle hand on Abby's shoulder. "Just remember, Abby, nothing's *ever* exactly the way you expect. Every new experience takes some adjusting to."

Abby wasn't listening. She glanced at her clock. "Only eighteen hours and seven minutes till BLAST-OFF!"

"Are you ever coming back?" Emily asked on the verge of tears. She was sitting forlornly on her tricycle and had been unusually quiet all afternoon.

"Of course I am, silly."

Emily's face brightened.

"I'll even write you—letters especially to you." Abby checked the clock again. "Now if only Merle would get here. We have to go through the movie magazines and decide which ones we're taking."

Merle was supposed to come over as soon as her dance lesson was over, but by five-thirty there was still no Merle, and no answer at her apartment. Then right before dinner, the phone rang.

"It's me," Merle's voice had a funny echo.

"I *know* that," Abby said. "Where have you been?"

Merle sounded like she was taking a deep breath. "You're not going to believe this," she said quickly, "but I'm at Lenox Hill Hospital. During dance class, I fell and broke my ankle."

"BROKE YOUR ANKLE?" Abby stared into the phone.

"I slipped when I pirouetted. The doctor just finished setting it. It doesn't hurt, but," Merle paused and continued in a small voice, "I'm going to be in a cast for at least *four* weeks."

"FOUR WEEKS! You poor kid." That was a shocker! But there was a bright side. "Hey, now you won't have to worry about any of the sports stuff at camp!" Abby couldn't help giggling at this strange stroke of good fortune. "Half the summer will be over before you even have to think about picking up a baseball bat."

There was another uneasy pause. "Abby, don't you see? . . . I can't go."

23

Abby was speechless. That was impossible. Just impossible.

"Abby, please don't be mad." Merle's voice was full of urgency. "It's not my fault, honest."

"Of course it's not," Abby mumbled, stunned. "I just don't understand is all."

"You know the whole reason my parents were so big on camp was because of all the outdoor stuff and now I can hardly walk, much less swim or do anything else. You know if it was up to me I'd still go just to be with you, but Mom already called Aunt Tillie. They're taking me to Cape Cod with them right before July Fourth weekend." Merle paused. "Hey, listen. This man's yelling 'cause he wants to use the phone. I'll call you as soon as I get home."

Abby mumbled goodbye and hung up.

"What is it, honey?" Ma had just come into the room. "You look like you just lost your best friend."

"Funny you should say that." Then Abby burst out crying.

4

"I DIDN'T expect so many kids," Abby said nervously. She was standing with Emily and her parents under the Pinecrest banner in the middle of the stifling hot bus terminal. All around her, screaming and waving to each other, were girls of every shape and size, each wearing the same green shorts and green blazer.

"I feel like I'm in the middle of a leprechaun convention," Daddy remarked.

Abby smiled weakly. If only her stomach would stop turning cartwheels. Daddy could joke about the girls but they didn't look at all funny to her. They looked impressive—especially the older ones whose blazers were covered with medals and ribbons. Abby wished her own glaringly new blazer didn't look so bare. Then she tugged at her hair. "Ma, can I see your mirror, please?"

"Honey, I keep telling you. You look *fine*." Ma dug down into her purse.

"I look awful," Abby wailed. "That haircut Mr. Bert gave me is gross. My hair looks like shredded wheat." Abby gazed at herself in Ma's mirror. Did she look like a fun-loving Pinecrest type, she wondered, or just a scrawny short kid with dark frizzy hair? What if nobody liked her? Abby felt as if she were setting forth into completely unknown territory. And she didn't like it. Not a bit.

"I know it's a big disappointment, Merle not coming." Ma squeezed her hand reassuringly. "But you'll see. The summer will turn out fine."

The whole point of the summer was to be with Merle, Abby thought to herself as she ducked out of the way of two girls who raced toward each other, hugging and shrieking. Best friends, obviously. They slapped their thighs, whirled around once, flapping their elbows like chicken wings, and clasped arms.

"The Pinecrest shake, I guess," Abby said. She'd seen lots of girls doing it. "Either that, or there's a new dance craze I missed."

"Now *that's* my girl," Daddy laughed. "Just keep your sense of humor and you'll be fine." That was what Daddy always told her. If you laughed and pretended everything was okay, you could usually fool yourself into believing it was true. Abby figured that was a pretty good way to be, only a lot of times she just couldn't fake it.

"Now, Emily, don't pull away from me," Ma was saying, and then she began rattling on about how Abby should remember to write Grandma and shouldn't forget to put in her bite plate each night.

Abby nodded without listening. Once again she rolled back yesterday's events and refilmed them in her mind. Merle's bus would get stuck in traffic and she'd miss her lesson. Or the dancing teacher would get sick and cancel the class. . . . The least little change and Merle would be here right now.

"Accidents happen, and there's nothing you can do about them," Ma had said last night but Abby didn't consider that any explanation at all. What was the point in making plans if you couldn't count on them?

She felt for the small wrapped package in her pocket. She and Merle had exchanged presents this morning. Her hand felt funny now without her small blue enamel heart ring, but Merle was always saying how much she loved it.

The big digital clock in the bus terminal suddenly clicked to 9:30, and in an instant the counselors began blowing their whistles. Everybody started grabbing for their suitcases and kissing their parents goodbye.

"This is it," Abby said. She took a deep breath and turned to Ma and Daddy.

Then without warning, Emily broke loose from Ma and bolted into the forest of Pinecrest campers.

"Where's she gone to now?" Ma looked worried and exasperated.

Daddy shouted for Emily who was not so easy to spot since she had insisted on wearing a white T-shirt and green shorts "just like Abby's" except that hers had a frog on the front pocket.

"Terrific," Abby fumed. "The kid sure has perfect timing."

"Sweety, we've got to find her." Ma sounded rushed and apologetic.

"Over there—I think I see her," Daddy shouted. They both grabbed Abby, smothered her with a fast hug and kiss, and were swallowed up by the crowd.

"Leave it to Emily." Forcing back angry tears Abby

headed toward the buses, carried along by the tide of campers.

"Abby! Wait!"

Good old Ma! Abby turned expectantly. She knew Ma couldn't leave. Not without a *real* goodbye.

"Your suitcase," Ma was yelling over the crowd. "You're leaving without your suitcase!"

Oops! Abby doubled back through the mob, grabbed her suitcase, then rejoined the crush of girls.

July 1
Dear Merle,

You are the very first person I'm writing, so feel honored. I miss you tons already. I have your locket on right now and I swear I'm not taking it off all summer. Are you wearing my ring?

Don't feel guilty but so far I'm miserable. Were you ever right about it being strict. There are rules for everything. Everybody is scared stiff of Aunt Tillie—even the counselors.

Some of the kids in my bunk are okay but there's nobody who is really on my wavelength (nobody with a warped enough mind, ha! ha!). There's only one other new kid besides me. Her name is Eileen. She's very sweet but shy and spends most of the time in the Nature Hut with her gerbils, Rudy and Trudy. Eileen's a vegetarian so she has special permission and doesn't have to eat meat which, if you ask me, is verrry smart because you should see the gross stuff they serve. Another kid, Lisa, seems okay but a real goody-goody. She's always first up at flag-raising, first to finish her job during cleanup, and is always buttering up the counse-

lors—you know the type. She was the prize camper for our group last year and I think she'll have a cow if she doesn't get it again this year. The other two girls, Phyllis and Bonnie, I really don't like. Phyllis is pretty but mean. She has long braids and looks sort of like Laura in "Little House on the Prairie." Bonnie is very tall with red hair that's even curlier than mine. Phyllis worships Bonnie and follows her around doing whatever dumb stuff Bonnie tells her. Yesterday they started making fun of Eileen who has a little lisp. I told them to cut it out so now they pick on me instead. This morning they put toothpaste on the toilet seat when I wasn't looking. And last night they frenched my bed. Hardy har! har!

One thing I have to say about Bonnie, she is really a great athlete. You should see her hit a softball. She's also the only one who sticks out in front and boy is she sensitive about it. She won't let anybody see her when she gets undressed.

The last kid who's named Roberta still hasn't shown up because she got chicken pox. She'll be here in about a week, but everybody says she's a creep anyway.

Our counselor Marty is no prize either. Most of the time she tries to act like we're invisible but sometimes she gets mean for no good reason. Like last night she took down all the snapshots Eileen had taped to the wall of her sheepdog, Ruggles. Marty said it was against the rules. Anyway, she tore one of the pictures and Eileen got very upset.

Oops! There goes the bell for dinner. I miss you sooo much. I hope your leg is feeling better. I'm glad I got to sign your cast. Please write S-O-O-N.

> Yours till Niagara Falls,
> Abby

July 1
Dear Ma and Daddy,

How are you? I am fine. The bunk I'm in is called Butter-cup. Be sure you put that on when you write. The girls in my bunk seem pretty nice. My counselor's name is Marty. She has a big rear end and bad skin but is all right. I miss you all a lot. Say hi to Emily. I'll write again soon.

Love,
Me

5

THE EVENING activity—charades in the Rec Hall—was over and Abby and Eileen were heading back to Buttercup. The whole camp was built on a steep hill covered with pines and graceful birch trees. At the top, which leveled off into a wide grassy field, were the tennis courts, the softball diamond, the arts and crafts shack, the Nature Hut, and the Rec Hall. Strung down along the side of the hill were the bunks, all named after flowers because Aunt Tillie expected her girls to "grow and blossom." And at the bottom was Lake Pocahontas.

Abby pretended to stagger the last few steps to Buttercup. "I'm beat. I swear I thought this day would never end," she said to Eileen. "Run up the hill for softball, run down to the lake for boating, run back up for archery." Abby put her hands on her hips and mimicked the counselors. " 'Abby Kimmel, that's not what *I* call rowing!' . . . 'Abby Kimmel, can't you run any faster than *that?*' " Abby made a face. "I'm gonna have a heart attack if they keep this up."

Eileen giggled shyly. "I wish they'd give us more stuff like nature and arts and crafts," she said in her whispery voice. "The only time I get to see my gerbils is during free period." Then she looked up at the sky. "But it sure is pretty here."

"Yeah. You never see this many stars in the city."
The inky expanse of sky certainly was beautiful but so
vast and deep that just looking at it sent a wave of loneliness through Abby. She gulped and blinked quickly.
"Where's the Big Dipper?" she asked to distract herself. "I can never find it." Abby began scanning the
black sky, trying to pick out the right stars, when she
heard Marty shouting from the bunk porch. "Inside,
you two!"

Marty was standing by the door, her chunky arms
folded, tapping her foot impatiently. "I thought I had
made it perfectly clear," she barked as Abby and Eileen
hurried down that path. "But in case I didn't, I will
repeat—in simple English: after evening activity, I want
you *straight* back here, and no dawdling."

"Geez, we're not late or anything," Abby said as she
was rudely hustled inside. That Marty. All she was interested in was getting to the counselors' shack where
she played cards with Josie who was some sorority sister
of hers from college. Abby remembered Marty's very
first words to the bunk. "Don't bug me and I won't bug
you. But give me trouble and I can get very nasty."

"Brush those teeth and then get undressed—on the
double!" Marty ordered now. "Everybody else is all
ready for lights out." Lisa, Bonnie, and Phyllis all
smiled self-righteously from their beds.

"Aye, aye, sir," Abby muttered under her breath.
Then she and Eileen hustled into the bathroom, tooth-
brushes in hand, smiling at each other in a conspiratorial
way.

"Hurry it up," Marty called in to them. "I'm turning

out the lights." Then Abby heard the door slam and the sound of footsteps crunching away.

"Brother, I sure am beat," she said as she and Eileen felt their way in the darkness to their beds. "I can't wait to hit the sack."

Bonnie, who had been strangely quiet until now, let out a little whoop and suddenly she and Phyllis broke up laughing.

Abby stopped at the foot of Bonnie's bed. "Did I miss something hysterical that I said?"

"Ooooh, noo," Bonnie said. "Sweet dreams."

Abby flopped gratefully into bed. The crisp sheets felt wonderful. Then she felt a creak, heard a squeak, and— CRASH—suddenly her bed collapsed on the floor, banging the back of her neck on the iron headbar.

"Abby! Are you okay?" Eileen asked while Bonnie and Phyllis clutched each other, doubled over with laughter.

"Some joke!" Abby exploded, rubbing her neck. "I could've really hurt myself."

"Don't look at us," Bonnie choked out between fits of giggling. "These cots are old. Maybe the hinges are weak."

"Or the screws could be loose," Phyllis chimed in.

"You—You—" Abby sputtered. "You just better cut this stuff out or—"

"Or what?" Bonnie had stopped laughing and there was a mean edge to her voice.

"Will you all kindly shut up," Lisa hissed. "Before some counselor comes in here and docks the whole bunk."

Fuming, Abby managed to get her bed back up, with Eileen's help. Then she got back into it, clamping her pillow over her head to block out the sound of Bonnie and Phyllis giggling.

July 2
Dear Merle,

I'm going to be in big trouble if the counselor on patrol catches me now. It's way after lights out and I'm writing under the covers with a flashlight. But I just had to write.

Tonight Bonnie and Phyllis collapsed my bed. Then when I was asleep they stuck my hand in a glass of water. It's supposed to make you pee but it didn't. When I yelled at them, the counselor on patrol told me to shut up or else I'd get docked (that means you have to miss evening activity and go straight to bed after dinner).

Daddy always says to keep a sense of humor. Maybe if I laughed it off, they'd quit bugging me. But I can't. I hate being picked on. If you were here, then it wouldn't be two against one.

I better sign off.

> *Love n mush,*
> *Abby*

P.S. Whatever you do, don't dare tell your parents a thing about me hating it here. I'm scared if Ma and Daddy find out the truth, they'll have a cow. They'd never listen to anything I wanted to do ever again. What a mess!

July 3
Dear Ma and Daddy,

    Thanks for your letter. I'm fine. Really. The reason my letters are short is because they don't give us much time to write, but I promise I'll try to do better. Don't worry, Ma. I won't forget to write Grandma.

Lots of love,
Me

July 3
Dear Merle,

    Camp's still bad. The only good thing is that I passed my first swim test. Now I'm what they call a goldfish. It was pretty cinchy stuff that I had learned at the Y ages ago but Eileen didn't pass so she's still a guppy and has to stay in the very shallowest water. Here is how the dock looks. Where the goldfish and guppies stay is called the Fish Bowl.

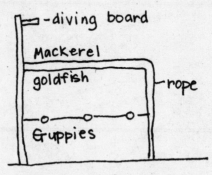

So far Bonnie is the only one in our group who's a mackerel. I'll probably get to be a mackerel pretty soon, but I can forget about becoming a dolphin. You have to dive off the diving board to be a dolphin. Do you remember how I almost killed myself that time at the Y when I tried it? No way am I doing that.

Thanks for filling me in on "Live for Today." I think Owen must be a moron not to realize Ben is his brother after all this time.

Write me the absolute first second you get to Cape Cod. Maybe you'll meet some stars and get your cast autographed! I miss you tons. Tomorrow we go to the beach for a July 4th picnic if it's nice.

> Yours till Porky Pig turns Kosher,
> Me

P.S. The last kid in our bunk, Roberta, still isn't here. Lisa told me last summer Bonnie and Phyllis did all these really mean things to Roberta—they even tried tying her to the flagpole one night. I guess it's cruddy of me, but I can't help feeling glad someone else will be around for them to bug.

6

A YELLOW BUS was waiting in front of the Rec Hall to pick up the girls from Buttercup and Bluebell. Laurel, the swimming counselor stood by the open door, clipboard in hand, busily checking off names as the girls climbed aboard.

"How's my new goldfish?" Laurel asked as Abby started to step inside.

Abby paused on the steps and smiled. "Glad to have the day off." She liked Laurel who always wore a white sailor cap and had lots of sun cream smeared on her peeling nose. Laurel had been the one to pass Abby on her swimming tests.

"Out of my way!" Bonnie shoved past her onto the bus and hurried to a seat that Phyllis was saving for her.

"Just watch the merchandise." Abby pretended to dust herself off as she climbed aboard the bus. Then she slid into the seat behind Bonnie and Phyllis, next to Lisa and Eileen.

"It looks like everybody is present and accounted for," Laurel announced a minute later. "So, we're off!"

The bus jounced out the entrance to camp and onto a dirt road with everybody singing "Ninety-nine Bottles of Beer On the Wall" at the top of their lungs. Abby saw Bonnie dig out a six-pack of Pepsi from her knapsack, pull off two cans, and pass one to Phyllis.

"Hey! You can't do that," Lisa protested, poking Bonnie in the back. "Those are supposed to be for lunch."

Abby rolled her eyes at Eileen. Lisa practically went into cardiac arrest if she saw somebody breaking a rule.

Bonnie turned and glared at Lisa. "What's it to you if I drink it now or later?"

"It's not fair," insisted Lisa, her cheeks reddening righteously. "The rest of us can't drink ours now. Why should you get to?" She started to squeeze out of her seat. "I'm telling Laurel."

"Okay, Lisa. Have it your way. I won't drink any." Bonnie said obligingly and she calmly proceeded to tip her can over Lisa.

"No, Bonnie, don't!" Abby cried out. She grabbed Bonnie's hand. Too late!

Bonnie and Phyllis clutched each other. Phyllis' braids bobbed up and down, she was laughing so hard.

"Yuck, yuck," Abby said sourly. A puddle of Pepsi was in her lap. Her T-shirt was sopping wet and soda was trickling down her legs.

"Come alive!" sang Phyllis. "You're in the Pepsi generation." And they both cracked up again.

"*What* is going on here?" Laurel sounded angry as she made her way to their seats.

"It was all Bonnie's fault," Lisa volunteered. "She started the whole thing."

Over loud protests, Laurel marched Bonnie to the

front of the bus. She returned with a Wash'n Dri for Abby. "When we get to the beach, you can really clean up in the restroom." Abby nodded miserably.

"Hey, watch it," Lisa whined. "You're dripping all over me."

Abby sat stewing, glaring at the back of Phyllis' head, wishing she had a pair of scissors to snip off those shiny braids. If only she didn't *always* let Bonnie and Phyllis get her! Eileen patted her consolingly, but Lisa didn't say another word. Talk about gratitude!

When only seven bottles of beer were left on the wall, the bus finally screeched to a stop and everybody clambered off. Abby saw a sign for the bathrooms, and she hurried through some bushes and thick tangly ivy until she reached the johns. She washed off as much of the stickiness as she could and then ran back to the group of girls who were all busy unpacking knapsacks on the beach.

"Now look, you guys," Laurel was saying. "I want everybody to put the food you've got in your knapsacks in here." She pointed to a Styrofoam cooler lying in the sand. "And the last person be sure and strap it up tightly."

That was Abby. She stripped down to her bathing suit, found her knapsack, then tossed in the bags of apples she'd been carrying, and joined everybody by the shore. Laurel was leading them out to the end of a long jetty. "This is called the 'easy chair'," she said, pointing to two massive flat-topped rocks, surrounded by railing, which led into the water like stone steps. "This beach is famous for it."

Overhead shrieking seagulls were patrolling the water and all around them the ocean churned furiously. Whenever a wave rolled in, it smacked and sprayed against the rocks. "So? Who's going to be first to sit back and relax?" Laurel surveyed the group. "Come on, don't be chicken. It looks scary but it isn't." There were still no volunteers. "All right then. I choose Eileen and . . . . . . Abby."

"Thanks a heap, Laurel," Abby groaned but deep down she hoped Laurel had picked her because she liked her.

Almost as soon as she squeezed in next to Eileen, the first wave crashed against her. "Wow! What hit me!" Abby spluttered. Eileen was coughing too and trying to rub salt water out of her eyes.

"Surprise!" Laurel laughed back behind them, where everyone else was standing safely. "The trick is to duck down."

"Now she tells me," retorted Abby, and as she watched the next big wave building, she clutched Eileen. They started shrieking and covering their eyes.

"Goodbye, cruel world!" Abby screamed. Then the wave loomed over them and down they ducked, letting the water thunder over their backs.

"Now you've got the hang of it," Laurel called.

"Don't look now," Abby yelled to Eileen. "Here comes another one!"

By the time she and Eileen got out of the "easy chair," dripping and shivering, everyone was shouting "Me next!" Laurel made sure everybody got two turns getting pulverized by the waves, then she ushered her wet, blue-lipped troop back to the beach for lunch.

"Lunch! You just said the magic word," Abby said, suddenly famished. Her teeth were chattering and she was practically numb with cold but it struck her that for the first time since she got to camp she was actually having fun.

"The salt air really works up your appetite," Laurel explained. Then she stopped dead in her tracks. "Oh, no!"

A crowd of shrieking seagulls were staging a riot around the Styrofoam chest, now open and dumped over on its side. Food was strewn everywhere—hot dogs, buns, tomatoes—all bitten into and coated with sand.

"Shoo!" Laurel shouted, running up and swatting at the birds with a towel. "Caw! Caw!" they cackled back, hopping up and down, flapping their wings.

"Hey, look over there," Abby poked Eileen. One seagull had a hot dog stuck like a cigar in its beak. "It looks like Groucho Marx!"

Abby grabbed for her towel to help fight off the birds but "Forget it," Laurel told the girls. "It's no use. All the food's ruined anyway. We might as well let them finish it. Then they'll go and we can get the cooler." Laurel glanced at her watch. "Shoot! We still have over an hour before the bus is supposed to pick us up."

"Oh cute," said Bonnie, plopping down in the sand. "So we have to sit here and starve until then?"

Laurel had Lisa call camp to send the bus for them right away. "What I can't figure out," Laurel said while they all sat up by the dunes, "is how those gulls got to the food." Her sun-creamed nose wrinkled in puzzlement. "They shouldn't have been able to. Not if the chest was properly closed."

Uh-oh, thought Abby, prickling with uneasiness. Laurel looked around the group. "Who did close it anyway?"

"I did," Abby said, nervously sifting sand through her fingers. "At least I think I did." She looked up warily. All of a sudden several pairs of hostile eyes were focused on her.

"Abby, don't you remember shutting it? Buckling the straps?" Laurel asked.

"Weeellll . . . actually no," confessed Abby, wishing the sand would just swallow her up. "Hey, lookit, Laurel and everybody. I'm really sorry. I just wasn't thinking. I always seem to do dumb stuff like this." Abby smiled sheepishly at the group, put a finger to her temple and pretended to pull the trigger. "Hey, come on. Please don't look that way. It's only lunch."

"Tell that to my stomach," said a girl from Bluebell.

"Well, I guess there's nothing we can do but wait till the bus comes," Laurel said flatly. She lay back and pulled her sailor cap over her eyes.

"You'll probably get docked for this," Lisa informed Abby.

Big deal, thought Abby glumly. What was getting docked compare with being hated by everybody? The first good time. And now it was spoiled . . . because of me, she couldn't help adding.

"Don't feel too bad," Eileen whispered softly. "I wouldn't have eaten most of the stuff anyway, being a vegetarian."

Abby smiled gratefully. If only everybody else would stop shooting her such dirty looks. Already Bonnie and Phyllis had their heads together whispering. Of course they couldn't do anything now with Laurel around but later they'd pull something to get back at her. Abby propped her chin on her hand and was miserably pondering her fate when suddenly there was a loud TOOT and everybody jumped up and started racing towards the yellow bus.

7

THE NEXT MORNING before reveille, Abby woke up with her face on fire. "What'd you do to me?" she screamed at Bonnie whose carrot top was buried under the covers.

"What?" Bonnie muttered groggily. She sat up and took a closer look at Abby. "Wow, it's the creeping crud!"

Abby bolted for the bathroom. She stared, horrified, into the mirror: only her blue-striped pajamas and nest of frizzy hair told her that the hideous reflection was her own. Her face was a swollen mass of tiny red bumps. Her eyes were no longer eyes, just puffy slits. And she itched. Oh, how she itched.

"What's wrong with me?" she wailed.

The camp nurse knew right away.

July 5
Dear Merle,
Guess who's in the infirmary with poison ivy? Yours truly got it yesterday taking a shortcut to the bathroom at the beach. I walked through a nice big clump of poison ivy. It sure wasn't my day. I also forgot to lock up the picnic food and a bunch of seagulls came and ate it all up. Now everybody in my group is ready to kill me. Nobody except Eileen is even speaking to me.

Be sure and keep those cards and letters coming. I can't wait to hear what Cape Cod is like. It's sure to be better than here. Boy, would I give anything to be with you. In fact I'd give anything not to be here.

> *Yours till Niagara Falls,*
> *Abby*

P.S. If you could see me, you'd scream. With all this Cala-mine plastered all over me, I look like the mummy in Curse of the Pharoahs.

P.P.S. Only 51 more days till I come home.

That afternoon Abby had company in the infirmary. Katy, the nurse, led in a sobbing girl with a mouth full of braces and deposited her on the bed next to Abby's. "You just rest a while, Gwendolyn," Katy said, "and you'll feel better." Gwendolyn was crying so hard it actually sounded like boo-hoo.

"What's wrong?" Abby whispered to Katy.

"Homesick." Katy mouthed the word as she swatted Abby's hand to keep her from scratching her poison ivy.

Abby looked over at the sodden heap on the bed bside hers. Poor kid, she thought. Gwendolyn probably hated camp as much as she did. Abby felt a sudden, fierce bond of kinship. "Gwendolyn, don't feel so bad," she said softly. "Join the club—I hate camp too. And I really thought it was going to be terrific."

"I *don't* want to talk," Gwendolyn said stiffly through her sobs. She turned away facing the wall.

"Okay, if that's the way you feel." Abby shrugged and picked up a comic book. "I was only trying to be friendly."

"Nobody's suppose to talk to you anyway," Gwen-

46

dolyn added. "Bonnie spread it around."

"Oh, swell! Do you have to listen to everything that moron says?" She glared at Gwendolyn's back. "Forget it. I don't feel like talking to you anyway."

Goodbye and good riddance, Abby muttered when Gwendolyn, still a sniffling, red-eyed mess, was let out before dinner. At least I'm not such a crybaby, for God's sake. And then seeing Katy wasn't around, Abby got in a few minutes of feverish scratching.

When she woke up the next morning Abby felt a little less itchy, a little less swollen, a little more cheerful. Hopping out of bed, she went to get her brush and the extra pajamas that Marty had sent down. She opened the bureau drawer, then let out a loud yelp.

"There's something in here," she screamed as Katy came rushing in, still in her bathrobe. "It looks like a hand . . . and it's *moving*."

"What in heaven's name are you talking about?" Katy proceeded carefully to the bureau and peered inside. She let out a low whistle, then yanked Abby by the arm and made her look too. "Honestly, Abby. I think you've seen too many horror movies."

"Wow!" was all Abby said. Nestled against her red polkadot pajamas was a small mouse about the size of her fist, surrounded by four—or was it five?—tiny pink babies, all squirming and wriggling and making soft chirping sounds.

"You know, they *do* sort of look like little wrinkly fingers," Katy chuckled. "I guess the mother wanted to find a nice, warm place to have her babies and decided your pajamas were just the spot."

47

"They're so—" Abby searched for the right word "—brand *new*. Do you think they'll stay here?"

Katy rubbed her chin thoughtfully. "I don't think that mother's going anywhere. Not just yet, at least."

After breakfast, Abby read through a book from the infirmary library called *Wildlife Pets*. The mice must be deer mice, she realized from the pictures, since the mother was tan—sort of the color of toast—and had a creamy white belly with dainty white feet. Several times Abby stopped to drop off snacks and peek in at the tiny brood. It amazed her how stone still the mouse lay while the babies drank her milk. And the skin on the babies. Abby couldn't get over it. It was so tissue-thin that when they nursed, she could actually see the milk gurgling around inside their stomachs.

"You think Bambi's a good name for the mother mouse?" asked Abby later on while Katy slathered her with another coating of Calamine lotion. "I thought of it because she's a deer mouse."

"That's a nice name," Katy answered recapping the bottle. "Those mice are lucky to have such a responsible girl looking after them."

Responsible! thought Abby. That's a laugh. But really it was nice to hear Katy say it anyway.

After dinner the infirmary phone jangled loudly.

Katy picked it up. "Hold on just one minute," she said and handed the receiver to Abby.

"Honey! How are you?" the familiar voice crackled over the phone.

"Ma!" Abby cried in a wavery voice.

"Aunt Tillie just called. Poor baby. What rotten luck.

Well, at least—No, Emily, you *can't* talk yet—at least, you'll be out soon. Do you feel just *awful,* honey?''

''Well, they just took me off the critical list,'' Abby said. If she didn't joke now, she knew she would burst out crying. Then she'd have to tell Ma and Daddy just how miserable she was.

''Now that's my girl,'' Daddy said, laughing. ''Boy do I miss you. The apartment seems so quiet. Neat, yes! But *awfully* quiet.''

That did it. Abby felt like a button had been pushed inside her. Her throat closed with the start of tears and, without meaning to, she spilled out everything. ''I'm so unhappy here,'' she wailed. ''I *hate* it. It's nothing like I thought it was going to be. It's so strict and everybody hates me.'' Abby rushed on. ''If only Merle were here.''

''But Merle isn't, and *you* are.'' Ma didn't sound angry or surprised, but she said firmly, ''You *must* learn to make the best of situations even when they don't turn out like you want.'' Then Ma's voice grew soft. ''Listen, honey. You don't think we like to see you unhappy, do you?''

''Then let me come home,'' Abby cried. There. She had said it.

''Now, Abby, stop it,'' Daddy said quietly. ''I don't want to hear talk like that. Who ever got anywhere by quitting? Look at Eleanor Roosevelt. Look at Golda Meir. Look at Fritzi Winkelhoff. . . .''

''Fritzi Winkelhoff? I never heard of her.''

''Of course you haven't—she's the one who quit!''

''Oh, *Dad*-dy,'' Abby groaned and sniffled. She

could feel the Calamine on her face getting all gooey from her tears. "You're a real wit. A—"

"Half-wit. I know, I know." It was an old joke between them. "But you think about it anyway. Now we're going to get off and put your sister on before she rips the phone out of the socket."

"Who poisoned you?" Emily asked right away.

"Nobody, silly." Abby reached for a Kleenex and honked into it loudly. "I have poison ivy. It's a rash and it makes you itch."

"Oh."

"Well, don't sound so disappointed."

"Abby, I get to sleep in your room now." Emily sounded triumphant. "Mommy said I could."

"You better be out by the time I come home."

"That's not for a *long* time."

"I know," said Abby miserably. "You don't have to rub it in."

A minute later, everybody said goodbye. Click. They were gone, and Abby felt a hundred times worse. I wish they hadn't called, she thought, making a beeline for her bed. She did not even stop to look in on the mice. If there were one thing she couldn't take right now, it was the sight of all that family togetherness.

8

THE NEXT MORNING Abby—and the mice—were released from the infirmary. Her charges were still nestled in the bureau drawer as Abby timidly entered Buttercup. The mice were so lovable. She hoped somehow they would help make up for the ruined picnic; she hoped they would become bunk mascots.

The bunk was empty except for Marty who was engrossed in a game of gin with Josie, the counselor from Bluebell.

"Everybody's at badminton," Marty informed Abby, not even bothering to look up from her cards. "And you'd better get over there, too."

"I will. Right away." Abby smiled her most winning smile. "But first I have a teeny favor to ask."

But Marty would hear none of it. She insisted Abby get rid of "those vermin" immediately.

"But Marty, please. PLLEEEEAASE. I swear they won't be any trouble. I'll take care of everything. You won't even know they're here."

Marty slammed down her cards and stared fiercely at Abby. "Don't make me say it again. Either those mice get dumped back of the bunk or you take 'em on up to the Nature Hut."

"Well, okay for you!" Abby huffed indignantly and

stormed off to the Nature Hut where Maya, the nature counselor was more than happy to put up with the new arrivals. They joined a menagerie that included a garter snake, several toads, an injured raccoon, and Eileen's gerbils, Trudy and Rudy, one of whom was running wildly in place on a little wheel in its cage. Maya told Abby that she could build a proper home for the mice to replace the drawer.

"Well, at least they're in good hands," Abby consoled herself as she trudged back to the bunk. She was not looking forward to her reunion with her bunkmates. As soon as they see me, she thought, Bonnie and Phyllis'll probably start screaming how I have cooties and— Abby stopped to scratch herself. Well, this time, she wasn't going to let them get to her. She straightened up and marched toward Buttercup.

"Welcome back, Abby," Eileen greeted her from the porch.

"I did your cleanup job all three days," Lisa announced. "Didn't I, Marty."

"I tried to come and visit you," Eileen whispered, "but Marty wouldn't let me."

Abby brightened. "Hey! You're gonna flip when you see what I brought to the Nature Hut. Your gerbils have new friends." Abby started to tell her all about the discovery when Bonnie and Phyllis sauntered out.

"Hi, you guys. I'm back!" Abby forced a smile. "Hope you didn't miss me too much!"

Bonnie looked right through Abby and turned to Phyllis. "Do you hear somebody saying something? Cause I sure don't."

Abby tried to stay calm. "Look, I'm sorry about the other day but—"

"I don't hear anybody either." Phyllis shook her head so that her braids danced. Bonnie smirked.

That did it. "The silent treatment!" Abby shouted, throwing up her hands. "Well, suits me fine. It'll be a *pleasure* not to have to talk to you."

Bonnie and Phyllis exchanged satisfied looks.

Just then a taxi roared down the hill sending up a spray of gravel in its wake. "Look!" Phyllis cried. "I bet it's her!"

The cab stopped in front of the bunk; the driver jumped out of the front seat and unloaded from the back seat one suitcase, one tennis racket and one girl in green shorts and a white T-shirt. With considerable relief, Abby realized her return was being upstaged by Roberta's arrival.

If ever anybody had the look of a born victim, it was Roberta. She was shorter than Abby and tubby, with round owlish eyes magnified by glasses that gave her an odd startled look as if someone had just yelled "Boo!" And all over her face and arms and legs were nasty-looking little scabs, the remnants of chicken pox. Bonnie and Phyllis were already exchanging sly looks and Abby felt a wave of sympathy as she watched Roberta wave goodbye to the cab. She trotted down the porch steps and made a move to help Roberta with her suitcase but Roberta just brushed her away and picked it up herself. "Don't bother," she said. Abby stepped aside, stung by Roberta's unfriendliness.

"Roberta. Ro-ber-ta," Bonnie sang out from the

porch. "We were wondering when you'd show up."

Abby tried to imagine what mean stuff Bonnie and Phyllis had planned. Well, too bad for Roberta. If she couldn't accept a simple gesture of kindness, Abby wasn't wasting any time feeling sorry for her.

Roberta marched up the steps past Bonnie and Phyllis. "Well here I am," she announced. "Back by popular demand." She nodded grandly at Lisa and Eileen then flung open the screen door—a little too hard—because it promptly swung back, thwacking her in the face. Roberta acted as if nothing had happened and proceeded inside. Abby giggled in spite of herself. Roberta was some klutz all right, but at least she had style.

"Same spaz as always." Bonnie followed her in. "You haven't changed a bit."

Roberta turned and smiled widely. "Maybe so, but you sure have. . . . Vavava*voom!*" she said, staring at the twin bumps under Bonnie's T-shirt.

Bonnie flushed and hunched her shoulders.

Abby's mouth fell open. Well, chalk one up for Roberta, Abby thought, shaking her head in grudging admiration. Talk about looks being deceiving! She spotted Roberta's suitcase open on her bed. Inside was practically nothing but candy and gum. Maybe there was hope for this kid yet!

At lunch Roberta seemed not exactly friendly, but less hostile. She informed Abby and Eileen that she was a Groucho Marx fan; had had appendicitis (with a scar to prove it); and lived outside Boston which accounted for the interesting way she spoke, calling their counselor "Maahty" and pronouncing "*Aunt* Tillie" "Ohnt."

"An 'ant' is an insect, not a relative," Roberta informed Abby. *"You're* the one with the accent."

Abby was intrigued by Roberta. She seemed so cool and independent. That afternoon when Marty herded them up to the shower house, Abby made a point of sharing a clothes hook with her.

"I can't believe it's your third summer here. How can you stand it?" Abby asked.

"It's not my idea. My parents dump me here while they travel," Roberta said matter-of-factly. "They're in Europe now."

"Oh," said Abby, not knowing what else to say.

Lisa was first into the showers. "Ouch!" she yelped. "The water's really hot."

Roberta took off her glasses and her robe and proceeded, stark naked, to test out other stalls.

"Cute, Roberta." Bonnie was enveloped in her towel. "Do we really have to look at your disgusting blubber?"

Roberta turned and smiled sweetly. "Not everyone can look like they belong in *Playboy*."

Chalk up another point for the kid, Abby thought, and, smiling, she stepped into a stall, drew the curtain, and pulled down on the shower cord which sent a hard spray of water raining down on her. Boy did it feel good to wash off all that grungy Calamine.

Bang! Abby heard the door to the shower house slam shut. It was probably Lisa. Typical of her to be finished before everybody else.

Then a minute later Eileen called out, "Abby, if Marty asks, I'll be at the Nature Hut." Bang! went the door again. Phyllis was next to leave, shouting out to Bonnie that she'd be waiting for her back at the bunk.

When Abby finally emerged, thoroughly scrubbed and slightly scalded, Roberta stuck her head out of the stall. "Don't go before you get me my glasses. I'm blind without them." She groped for the glasses Abby handed her and wrapped her robe around her. It was then that they noticed one bathrobe still hung from a peg on the wall and one towel was draped over a shower stall still spitting out hot water.

Roberta checked inside the robe. Bonnie Unger, the nametape said. Her eyes brightened behind her foggy glasses.

"Are you thinking what I think you're thinking?" Abby asked in a whisper that barely contained her glee.

Roberta nodded. Quickly she tossed Abby the robe and yanked the towel from the shower stall. Bonnie poked her head out, trying to figure out what was happening.

Roberta waved to her.

"Ta! Ta!" said Abby.

Bang! went the shower house door.

"I can't wait till she gets back," Roberta said. They were back at the bunk lying in wait for Bonnie.

"Me neither," Abby giggled. "You don't think it was *too* mean, do you?"

Roberta looked at her. "Are you kidding? Bonnie's probably mad she didn't think of doing it to us first."

Soon Bonnie came flying toward the bunk, a shower curtain wrapped around her.

"She looks homicidal!" said Abby.

"Of all the MEAN, ROTTEN, LOW-DOWN—" Bonnie shouted.

"Smile!" said Roberta, whipping out her camera and snapping the shutter. Then she and Abby raced out of the bunk and kept running until they couldn't hear Bonnie bellowing anymore.

"Did you get a load of the look on her face?" Abby said when they stopped to catch their breath.

Roberta nodded with satisfaction. "Only we better keep away from the bunk until she calms down a little— that is if I want to make it to my eleventh birthday." Roberta thought for a moment. "Hey, let's go to the counselors' shack. We can spy on them."

That idea appealed to Abby immensely. The counselors' shack, which was deep in the woods by the lake, was strictly off-limits to campers. Abby didn't know anyone who had actually seen it, but there were all sorts of tantalizing rumors about the place—especially that counselors from the boys' camp across the lake were always sneaking over. It would be great to see what really went on.

"What are we waiting for?" Abby began running after Roberta into the woods. Then she remembered. The Nature Hut. She'd told Maya she'd come and start building a home for the mice during free period. Well, that could probably wait, Abby figured, and anyway, Eileen would be around if there was anything that *had* to be done. Then Abby felt a funny pang in her stomach, which she thought was a pretty odd place for her conscience to strike.

"Roberta, I forgot. I'm supposed to be at the Nature Hut now. I have these mice—Hey! Why don't you come too?"

"Nah, I don't like animals and the feeling is mutual."

"You'll like the mice," Abby insisted. "They're adorable."

"But I've never been to the counselors' shack," Roberta said. "Every summer I plan to sneak over and then somehow I never do."

"I'll go with you another time, I promise." Abby gently pulled Roberta in the direction of the Nature Hut. "After all," she smiled at her new friend, "we've got the whole summer."

July 10
Dear Ma and Daddy,

Guess what? I'm a mackerel. That's the second best in swimming and means now I get to go out way over my head. Don't worry, Ma. It's very safe—nobody's drowned yet (that was a joke!).

Here is more good news. The last girl in our bunk finally got here. She came late because she had chicken pox. Her name is Roberta Harrison. I like her best of anybody in the bunk (she likes me best too). I already told her she could hang around with us on Parents' Visiting Day because her parents won't be here.

Roberta has more accidents than anybody I ever met. So far she has fallen out of bed, gotten a nosebleed from being hit with a volleyball, and tipped over backwards in her chair during dinner. Everybody in the Mess Hall started banging their spoons when she crashed. I would have died if it had been me, but Roberta just got up and announced, "And now for my next trick!"

Did I tell you about my mice? I think I forgot to when you called. I found a whole family of them in the infirmary and now I keep them in the Nature Hut. The babies are only a few days old and already they're growing all this soft fur. They are so cute. Me and this kid Eileen fixed up a nice cage out of an aquarium with lots of stuff for them to play with. At the end of the summer I get to take them home if it's okay with you. Please say yes.

Well, that's all for now. Please send me some gum. Just sneak a few loose sticks in each letter.

Also make sure Emily is out of my room by the time I get home.

Love and a million kisses,
Me

July 12
Dear Merle,

I just got your letter. I feel awful, but I bet things get better at the theater. You always end up having fun wherever you are. That Nancy sure does sound like a snob. I never even heard of her mother—what movies has she been in anyway?

I almost feel guilty telling you this, but camp is getting better. It's weird how things change, isn't it? The last kid came and she's a lot of fun. Don't worry, though, you're still my best friend forever and ever. Numero uno!

Remember I wrote you about the mouse babies? I have one picked out for you. Its name is Fred Astaire because he (or she, I'm not exactly sure) sort of dances around a lot. Fred can even do somersaults. I swear I'm not kidding. It's hysterical to see. Roberta won't go near the mice anymore since one of them made in her hand. It was gross.

Well, free period is almost over so I'll sign off. I miss you tons. When is your cast coming off? Is there any chance your parents would let you come to camp for the second month?

Yours till Niagara Falls,

Abby

P.S. I learned a lot of new stuff in jacks. I'll show you when we get home. I can almost flip with one hand now.

July 12

Dear Grandma,

Thanks a lot for sending me the salami from Sol's Deli. I guess Ma didn't tell you but it's against the rules for us to get any food packages. It was very nice of you anyway. The food here is awful. Yesterday I found a spider in my chicken but at least it was dead.

I miss you, Grandma. Ma sent me a book of crosswords, but it's more fun doing them with you.

Love,

Abby

July 12

Dear Emily,

I'm glad you like your play group so much. Ma wrote me that Benjamin from upstairs is in it, too. I hear you kissed him. If I were you I'd cut out that kind of stuff.

I'm making you something in arts and crafts but I won't tell you what it is. It'll be a surprise when I come home.

Love from your sister,

Abby

P.S. You better not wreck any of the stuff in my room, and don't draw in any of my books. I mean it!

9

"GIRLS! I HAVE an announcement!" The sound of Aunt Tillie's voice produced a sudden hush in the noisy Mess Hall. "Tomorrow morning all regular activities are canceled." Excitement rippled through the room.

"I hope it's something good," Abby whispered, trying to spread her prune whip around the edges of her dish so it would look like she'd eaten some.

"Don't hold your breath," Roberta whispered back.

"Now, girls, take a close look at the color of your bunkmates' eyes," Aunt Tillie instructed, "because tomorrow morning the Blue Eyes and the Brown Eyes will be competing in—a swim meet!"

"Oh, goody," exclaimed Lisa as the camp erupted in cheers.

Roberta groaned.

"Rats," said Phyllis. "Now I can't be on the same team as you, Bonnie."

"Do we *have* to be in a race?" Abby asked Marty. Being in swimming races always made her stomach feel like it was doing back flips and her legs like they had turned to spaghetti.

"Yup, that's the rule. I've got the list right here." Marty fished a piece of paper from her blazer pocket. "For the Blue Eyes: Eileen is in the Ping-Pong race, Roberta's in the Potato Hunt—"

"I knew it. I get stuck in that every year."

"—and Phyllis is in the medley relay. For the Brown Eyes: Bonnie's in the 100-meter freestyle, Lisa's in the medley relay, and Abby's in the Cracker and Whistle."

"I think I got off pretty easy," Abby said later to Roberta and Eileen on their way to the Rec Hall for evening activity. As Roberta had explained, all Abby had to do for her race was swim one lap, climb on the dock, eat a cracker, then whistle and swim back.

Abby sucked in her cheeks, curled her tongue and let out several tweets. Nothing wrong with that whistle, she assured herself.

"Keep it up, Abby. Practice makes perfect," Bonnie called out tauntingly from behind her. Then she and Phyllis both started whistling loudly.

"Go ahead and make fun," Abby retorted, her hands on her hips. "But you won't be laughing tomorrow when I win the race."

"We'll see," Bonnie smiled.

Abby felt like a Grade-A jerk as she watched Bonnie saunter off arm-in-arm with Phyllis. "Me and my king-size mouth," she muttered. "What'd I have to go and say that for?" She kicked a pebble in frustration. "Now if I *don't* win, Bonnie'll never shut up about it."

"Don't worry. You're a good swimmer," Eileen said with quiet reassurance. "I bet you can win."

"Think positively," Roberta advised, and then she started up the song that was their current camp favorite:

Great green globs of greasy grimy gopher guts
Mutilated monkey meat

Little birdy dirty feet
Great green blobs of greasy grimy gopher guts
And I forgot my spoon!

It was a perfect morning for a swim meet, thought
Abby. The sun hung high in the sky like a shiny gold
medal and the lake was clear and calm.

Still practicing her whistle, Abby sat down on the
Brown Eyes side of the Fish Bowl. Both teams were
already cheering madly. Two of the Brown Eyes from
Sunflower, the oldest bunk, stood with their arms crossed, clasping hands. Seated in the human swing they
made was a small girl whom they tossed into the air
over and over again.

"Baby in the high chair," screamed the Brown Eyes,
"Who put her up there?
Ma! Pa! Sis Boom Bah!
Brown Eyes, Brown Eyes, Rah, Rah, Rah!"

The Blue Eyes answered back with their own deafening
cheer:

"When you're up, you're up
And when you're down, you're down.
But when you're up against the Blue Eyes
You're upside down!"

Then Aunt Tillie, perched atop a lifeguard chair in the
sand, blew her whistle and announced the first race.

"Will the girls in the Potato Hunt please assemble on shore," her voice blared over the bull horn.

Abby watched as Roberta and several girls, almost all guppies, turned their backs to the lake while one of the counselors tossed a bagful of potatoes into the Fish Bowl.

"Show'em who's champ!" Abby shouted to Roberta as she scrambled into the water with the rest of the Potato Hunters.

"Ab-*by*. I think you might try rooting for *our* side," Lisa snapped, sounding like a prim little schoolteacher.

"Way to go!" Abby screamed as Roberta deposited her first potato on shore.

By the end of the race Roberta had amassed a total of seven. That's showing them, Abby thought to herself as Aunt Tillie announced the winner of the Potato Hunt and presented a stunned Roberta with her swimming medal.

Roberta's unexpected victory boosted Abby's confidence. If Roberta can do it, so can I, she thought, closing her eyes and picturing herself receiving a shiny gold medal of her own for her blazer. "Two, four, six, eight!" the Brown Eyes would cheer for her.

Her heart pounding in anticipation, Abby watched the next races until finally the names of the girls in the Cracker and Whistle were announced over the bull horn. Abby waited at the edge of the dock next to the other contestants, arms back, ready to spring.

The whistle blew and in she jumped, because she was afraid to dive. What time she lost she quickly made up, plowing through the water with quick, sure strokes, her arms pumping up and down, her legs kicking in steady rhythm.

The first to reach the other side, Abby scrambled up the slats of the dock to the excited cheers of her teammates. Quickly she snatched a cracker from the counselor who was to judge her whistle and stuffed it into her mouth. Out of the corner of her eye, Abby nervously watched the other three girls climb out of the water and go to work on their crackers. She held the lead but only by a little.

Abby chewed furiously. Swallow! she commanded her throat, but her throat would not obey. The dry bits of cracker refused to go down. Abby chomped harder. Still she couldn't swallow. It was like trying to force down a gigantic wad of glue. Nothing to worry about, she told herself. Just stay calm, forget swallowing and whistle.

That was easier said than done, she soon discovered. With her mouth stuffed full of gummy cracker all that came out was a pathetic whooshing sound—like air being let out of a tire.

Growing more and more nervous, Abby soon heard a faint but unmistakable tweet from the girl next to her who, after getting the okay from her judge, dove back into the water.

She's beating me! Frantic, Abby pursed her lips again and blew with all her might. Instead of a whistle out flew a mouthful of wet cracker crumbs which sprayed her judge in the eye.

The judge looked startled, then amused. Carefully wiping off her face, she stomped her foot and wagged a finger in mock disapproval, as if Abby had actually spit on her on purpose.

The campers laughed long and hard at this unexpected comedy and before she had time to think better of it, Abby rashly tried whistling again. Again she blew cracker all over the judge's face. Again the campers screamed with laughter.

Mortified, Abby heard the splash of the other two girls who were starting on their return trip. *The only one left! I'm the only one left!* Abby let out a panicky wheeze which her judge seemed to interpret as a whistle—either that, or else she just took pity on her—because suddenly she signaled for Abby to swim back.

By the time she climbed out of the water the girls in the next race were already lined up. As inconspicuously as she could, Abby slunk back to her team's side of the dock and sat with her knees scrunched up to her chest, waiting for the swim meet to end. The instant the Brown Eyes were announced winners, she scuttled off the dock.

"Wait up, will you," Abby heard Roberta call from behind. Abby kept on walking up the hill but Roberta came panting up beside her. Abby couldn't help fixing her eyes enviously on the shiny gold medal pinned to Roberta's robe. "Hey, congrats! You were terrific," Abby said with as much cheer as she could muster. "I was rooting for you the whole time."

"Oh, it was nothing," said Roberta, blowing on her fingers and rubbing her medal. "You weren't bad yourself."

"Oh, yeah." Abby rolled her eyes.

"Listen. Groucho would have been proud. I bet he didn't always get laughs like that."

"You're just trying to make me feel better. I *hate* looking like such an idiot." Then, almost in spite of herself, Abby started to laugh. "Did you get a load of my judge's face? She didn't know what hit her!"

"Great play, Shakespeare!" Bonnie called out from behind. "Too bad we can't have a repeat performance."

Phyllis and some other girls near her started giggling.

Abby felt herself stiffen but forced her mouth into something resembling a smile. "Thank you, fans. Thank you." Abby bowed deeply as if she were taking a curtain call.

"Let's hear it again for the little lady!" Roberta said, clapping.

Then Abby swung an arm around Roberta. Funny, but in an odd way, Abby felt almost as if she had won a medal. She marched up to the bunk, swinging her bathing cap and singing as loud as she could, "Great green globs of greasy grimy gopher guts . . ."

10

THREE DAYS of rain, rain, rain, and no sign of it stopping. Jack tournaments and relay races were scheduled in the Rec Hall; an old Lucille Ball movie was shown in the playhouse—until a bat flew down from the rafters and stopped the performance; and a costume party was held in the Rec Hall with second prize awarded to Abby who, dressed in black leotard and tights with a pillow over her head, had come as a toasted marshmallow.

Now on the morning of the fourth straight day of bad weather, Abby sat cross-legged on the floor of Buttercup. She and Eileen were fitting together a jigsaw puzzle of Mount Rushmore that Ma had sent up. Abby looked out the splattered window and listened to the rain outside. It beat down on the roof of the bunk in a steady rhythm. Ratta-tatta. Ratta-tatta. Like the drum at campfire. It was a comforting sound, one that made her happy to be safe inside the snug, dry cabin. If only more days could be like this, thought Abby, while she hunted for the piece with George Washington's nose. No rushing off from one activity to the next! Imagine! The whole morning free except for compulsory shampoos.

Marty nabbed Roberta first.

"But I'm just getting over a cold. I might have a relapse," Roberta whined as Marty steered her into the bathroom.

"I have some business I have to attend to at the camp office," Marty informed them when she reappeared. "I want you all looking beautiful by the time I get back." Then she grabbed her slicker and dashed out into the pouring rain.

"A likely story," Bonnie muttered from her bed.

"She must think we're a bunch of morons," added Phyllis who was giving Bonnie a back rub. "As if we didn't know she's going to the counselors' shack."

"What goes on there anyway?" Eileen asked.

"Nobody knows because nobody's ever seen it," Lisa piped up. "It's against the rules for campers to go there. And it's also against the rules for a counselor to leave us alone in the bunk. We could report her."

"Only *you* would think of that," snapped Bonnie and for once Abby had to agree.

A minute later the noise of running water stopped and the bathroom door swung open to let out a cloud of steam. Roberta emerged, her hair dripping down in wet wormy strands. "Here she comes, Miss Amer-ic-a! Here she comes, your i-deal," she sang, dousing herself with baby powder.

"Hey, cut it out," cried Abby from the floor. "You're getting that stuff all over me."

Roberta shook her can harder. "Whatsamatter, sweet-cakes! Don't you want to smell good, too?" she drawled in a poor imitation of a southern accent.

"Okay, you asked for it!" Abby grabbed the powder can. Up she sprang, scattering puzzle pieces, and began chasing Roberta around the bunk, dousing her with powder whenever she got close enough to strike.

"Abby, come on. Cut it out," Lisa whined, peering out the window. "Marty'll be back and you'll get us in trouble."

"Trouble? Who cares? Live dangerously, I always say!" Abby turned on Lisa, showering her with powder, leaped over the bed to sprinkle Eileen, and then emptied the can on Bonnie and Phyllis.

In a flash, everyone—except Lisa—dashed into the bathroom to arm themselves with cans of powder.

The war was on.

Bonnie charged at Abby, powdering her in the eyes so that for a moment she couldn't see.

"My eyes! My eyes!" she yelped, burying her face in her arm.

For a half-second a worried look crossed Bonnie's face. "Gotcha!" Abby cried, grabbing Bonnie's can and going to work on her. "The oldest trick in the book and look who fell for it!"

Furious, Bonnie yelled, "I'll get you for that, Abby Kimmel," and she began swatting her with a pillow.

"Roberta to the rescue!" Another pillow whizzed across the bunk.

"Charge!" hollered Phyllis joining the fray.

"Have no fear; Eileen is here!"

In no time a layer of powder mixed with chicken feathers covered the bunk like a light snowfall and still the fight showed no signs of letting up.

"Come on," screamed Abby after she finished powdering everything of Marty's she could find—her bed, her books, her clothes. "Let's attack Bluebell!"

Everyone scrambled for the door. They got no farther.

There on the porch stood Aunt Tillie in a dripping poncho. She did not look amused.

"*Girls!* What is going on here?" Nobody said a word as Aunt Tillie marched into the bunk and, like a little general, inspected the wreckage. Abby just looked down at her feet and shifted her weight uncomfortably. "Well, I suppose it's perfectly clear what has been going on," Aunt Tillie said wryly. Abby stole a quick glance at her. Was there a faint hint of amusement in her voice?

Lisa raised her hand as if she were in class. "I wasn't in on it, Aunt Tillie. Honest!"

"I'm not interested in who was in on it." Aunt Tillie's voice was sharp again. No brownie points for Lisa that time. "What I care about is cleaning up this mess and seeing it doesn't happen again." She frowned and pursed her lips. "You're all very lucky. This sort of horseplay usually ends with somebody getting hurt."

Just then Marty walked into the bunk and her mouth dropped open.

"Wouldn't you know it. I'm gone one minute and look what happens," she scolded, as if only a dire emergency would have dragged her from the bunk.

Aunt Tillie gave Marty a long look and said she wanted to speak to her outside on the porch.

"I bet Marty really gets it now," Abby whispered. "Aunt Tillie's no dope."

"If Marty gets fired, maybe I'll get to keep Trudy and Rudy here at the bunk," Eileen said hopefully.

Bonnie snorted. "Don't you *ever* think about anything but those dumb gerbils—"

Bonnie shut up fast. Marty was back in the bunk, her lips pressed together and a grim look in her eyes, but she pretended that nothing had happened.

"Well, I hope you're all satisfied now." She slung her wet slicker on a wall hook and faced them squarely. "You will spend the rest of the day cleaning up this mess and then right after dinner, you're all docked. You are going straight to bed and will miss the counselors' serenade."

"Oh, no! Not that!" Roberta clutched herself in shocked disbelief. She sounded as though they had all been sentenced to fifty years on the rack.

Abby sucked in her breath. Roberta was going too far this time.

"Don't push me, Roberta." Marty's face reddened. "You all think you're so clever. Well, wait until you've finished cleaning up the bunk and then ask yourself if it was worth it."

Abby did as she was told. After hours of sponging and sweeping and dusting away powder and feathers, she wondered how what had taken only minutes to do could take so long to undo. Everyone complained loudly and bitterly but it struck Abby that for the very first time, there was a kind of spirit in the bunk. Maybe not of friendship, she realized, but at least of unity. We all got in trouble together. And we're all paying for it. Together.

When dinner was over, the exhausted inhabitants of Buttercup trundled back to the bunk where they gratefully collapsed into bed. Right before she fell asleep, Abby remembered to ask herself if it had been worth it.

With her nose buried in her pillow that still smelled sweetly of baby powder, Abby smiled drowsily. Yes . . . it had.

July 19
Dear Merle,

It sure would be nice to get some mail (hint, hint). Do you know it's a week since I got a letter from you? Please write, and that means now.

> *Yours till bacon strips,*
> *Abby*

P.S. Ma and Daddy are coming up this weekend (Emily has to stay at Grandma's, sob!). It seems like a million years since I've seen them—and you too.

July 19
Dear Ma and Daddy,

Please don't pay any attention to that letter Aunt Tillie sent about not bringing up any candy or junk on Visiting Day. Roberta told me the same letter gets sent every summer and all the parents bring up tons of junk anyway.

I can't wait to see you. In case you forgot what I look like(ha! ha!) here is a picture. Don't worry. My hair hasn't really turned gray. This was taken right after our bunk had a powder fight.

> *Love,*
> *Me*

I can't wait for you to see the mouse babies. They all have soft fur now and look like giant pussy willows. They are so cute. Mostly I can't wait for you to meet Roberta. I can't tell whether she minds about her parents not coming. She says she couldn't care less, but I don't know.

11

"THEY SHOULD BE here soon," Abby said excitedly to Roberta. From the bunk porch she impatiently watched the long caravan of cars inching down the hill to park on the flagpole field. "That's unless Daddy got lost. He's not too good with directions."

"Bunny-rabbit! We're here!" A tall red-headed mother came running toward the bunk, arms outstretched and Bonnie charged.

" 'Bunny-rabbit?' " Abby snorted and collapsed against a porch railing. "Gimme a break!"

Roberta didn't laugh. She was sitting on the porch steps studiously braiding a lanyard. All morning she'd been quiet and moody and her asthma had been acting up.

Abby looked down at the top of Roberta's bent head. "It's gonna be a good day, Roberta," she said. "I've got it all planned." She ticked off the activities on her fingers. "First we'll go on the picnic, then later we'll go swimming—we'll have loads of fun."

"Who said we wouldn't?" There was an unusual edge to Roberta's voice. "Lookit, I'm going down to the infirmary. I need another asthma pill."

"I'll come with you."

"No! You stay here. It won't take me long." Roberta

wrapped up her lanyard, pushed her glasses up on her nose, and stalked off.

"Hey, what's with her?" asked Lisa who arrived with her parents in tow.

Suddenly Abby felt cranky and irritable too. "Oh, just mind your own beeswax!" She sank down on the porch steps and thought about how rotten she'd feel if her parents weren't coming. But Roberta wouldn't even admit that was what was bothering her. Abby stared off moodily into space so that it took her a minute to focus on the familiar figures coming down the hill, peering at the signs on each bunk.

"Ma! Daddy!" she shrieked. "Here I am!" Abby flew up the hill, practically tackling her mother, jumping into her father's arms, hugging and kissing them until she was out of breath.

"Wow!" Daddy laughed. "If I didn't know better, I'd say you missed us."

"Ooooooh! It's so good to give you a big squeeze," Ma said, hugging Abby again. "You look great." She held her at arm's length. "A little thinner maybe but great." Then Ma's brow wrinkled. "Abby, how much weight *have* you lost?"

"Ma-*aaaa*. Come on, don't start in already," Abby said, feeling a strange mix of contentment and annoyance. Here they were. Daddy with his dumb jokes; Ma worrying. Just like old times.

At the bunk they dropped off the candy they had brought and waited for Roberta.

"*You* made this bed?" Ma said.

"Don't look like you're going into cardiac arrest. We

77

have to keep stuff neat. Otherwise we get marked off in inspection and lose candy privileges."

"*Verrry* interesting," said Ma. Abby hoped she wasn't getting any ideas.

"Hey, listen, Ab," Daddy said impatiently. "How long are we going to wait in here? I didn't drive all the way up here to sit in your bunk. I came to see you and the camp—in that order. Besides, we've got the whole day to find your friend."

"Daddy, please. Don't be that way," Abby said, hanging on her father's arm. "I thought you'd *want* to meet Roberta right away."

Ma smoothed Abby's hair. "Daddy didn't mean it like that. But I'm sure if you show us around, Roberta will turn up somewhere along the way." Ma took her hand and made motions toward the door. Reluctantly, Abby let herself be dragged out of the bunk. It wasn't fair. Ma and Daddy made such a big deal about being considerate. Why was it, Abby wondered, they could never see when *they* were being selfish?

Each stop of the tour was faithfully recorded by Daddy's camera. *Click*. Abby smiled self-consciously from a rowboat. *Click*. Abby posed with Ma who was wearing the pumpkin seed necklace Abby had made in arts and crafts. *Click*. A group portrait of Abby and the mice. Then right before lunch, as they headed back to the bunk to drop off the camera, Abby finally spotted Roberta on the porch of Buttercup. She broke loose from her parents. "Hey, where have you been?"

"I could say the same thing." Roberta was braiding her lanyard again.

"Come on, Roberta. That's not fair." Abby put a tentative hand on her friend's shoulder. "I waited for you. Only you didn't show—"

Daddy broke up their conversation. "I bet this is the little lady from Beantown," he said, coming up behind Abby and pumping Roberta's hand.

"*Dad*-dy. You promised you wouldn't act dumb."

"I feel like I know you already," Ma added. "All Abby's letters talk about is Roberta, Roberta, Roberta."

Roberta smiled in an uncharacteristically self-conscious way. She mumbled about how nice it was to meet them and then she folded up her lanyard and followed Abby and her parents down to the lake for the camp picnic.

"So, you still haven't told me where you disappeared to," Abby said, trying not to sound concerned. "Ve haf vays uff making you talk, you know."

Roberta smiled mysteriously. "Oh, I was just hanging around, watching the action." Then Roberta peered at Abby from behind her glasses and giggled a little. "You missed out on some good stuff."

"Yeah? Like what?" It was hard for Abby to tell if Roberta really had cheered up or was just faking it.

"Lisa's parents didn't bring up any candy," Roberta said, "but they did bring a present from Bloomingdale's for Marty."

"Bribery!" Abby cried in mock horror. "She'd do anything to get picked prize camper again."

"And Eileen's parents sneaked in Ruggles for a little while."

Abby laughed. For a month she'd been hearing stories

79

about Eileen's sheepdog.

"He's really cute and shaggy but get this," Roberta continued, really warming to her topic. "Just when Phyllis finished dumping out all her candy on her bed, Ruggles smelled it and attacked. He ate up nearly all her junk. Phyllis almost had a fit."

"A *fit?* I'm surprised she didn't attack the dog!"

Roberta laughed and Abby thought happily that Roberta really did seem like her old self. A minute later they reached the lakefront which was already aswarm with parents and campers staking out their territories for the picnic lunch. Eileen was waving at them frantically. She had saved a nice grassy spot by a shade tree and as soon as the counselors passed out the box lunches, everybody began feasting on fried chicken, corn on the cob and blueberry muffins. "This is absolutely delicious," Ma said between munches. "There is no reason in the world for you to be losing weight, Abby. Not with food like this."

"You don't *really* think they feed us like this every day? Roberta, you tell her."

But Ma wasn't listening. "Here, before I forget." She dug into her purse and handed Abby a snapshot. "Emily's summer play group put on a street carnival last Sunday and look who was the star of the freak show."

"The bearded lady!" Abby laughed when she saw the picture of Emily staring solemnly from behind a long black crepe paper beard. Abby thought her brain had to be going soft because suddenly part of her was almost wishing Emily was there.

"She's really cute," said Eileen.

Roberta leaned over. "Gee, from the way you talked, I was expecting a real frea—"

Abby nudged Roberta hard. "Did you bring any other pictures, Ma?"

No, but Ma did have a letter from Merle's mother. Abby grabbed for the envelope, hoping for some explanation for Merle's not writing. "It's weird. At first I was getting tons of letters," she said, "but now I haven't heard from her in ages." Abby skimmed over all the boring stuff about weather and shopping until she got to the heart of the letter.

We are all well and happy, it said. *At first Merle wasn't too keen on the place but now she's friends with a daughter of Kay Langton, the actress, and all's fine. Nancy is a year and a half older so, of course, Merle is flattered that she pays any attention to her. She's been begging me for days to let her get her ears pierced like Nancy's so yesterday, when her cast come off, I finally gave in.*

Abby read on in disbelief. That kid Nancy. Hadn't Merle said she couldn't stand her? "I don't get it," Abby said. "Merle sounds so different in this letter." Piercing her ears. How gross! What if Merle was all different when they got home? Then what?

"Come on, honey. It sounds like Merle was very unhappy at first. I'd think you'd be happy that she has a friend."

"Well, I am. I guess." But not, thought Abby, if it meant *their* friendship was going to change. That *had* to stay the same. Forever.

Abby was still brooding when Marty appeared carrying a big package with lots of foreign stamps on it. "Here, this just came for you." She deposited the box into Roberta's lap.

With little interest, Roberta tore off the wrappings. There, inside a fancy silver paper box, nesting in a bed of fake straw, were six china eggs with delicate blue and yellow flowers painted on them.

"Ooh, Roberta. Those are really pretty," Eileen breathed, although Abby couldn't help thinking they looked more like the sort of present she'd buy her mother.

Ma popped the top off an egg. Inside were crumply rose-gray petals that smelled nice. "This is called potpourri," she said, holding the egg to her nose. "It's dried flowers mixed with spices."

Roberta arched an unimpressed eyebrow. "What they sent last year was better."

Abby saw Ma shoot Daddy a funny look.

"I think I'm going to leave them in the bunk for now," Roberta got up. "I'll give one out to everybody later."

When Roberta didn't come back, Abby said, "Look, I have to go to the bunk for something too."

She found Roberta lying face down on her bed. Next to her was a little white card that said, *Italy awfully hot but fun. We're off to San Remo tomorrow. Hope you and your bunkmates like the present. Love, Mother and Dad.*

"Roberta," Abby said. Roberta's face shot around. She quickly put on her glasses to cover her red eyes. "My asthma started bothering me." Roberta gave a little wheeze, then clutched at her throat. "But it's nothing serious, Doctor." She pretended to choke and bulge out her eyes.

Abby didn't laugh. She groped to find the right thing to say. Then suddenly she realized Roberta did not want her to say anything at all. If it was me, Abby thought, I'd tell her how *I* feel. But Roberta was so different. She hardly ever talked about her parents and when she did it was always in a joking way, calling them Jack and Teddy. Daddy's wrong, Abby decided. You couldn't always keep your sense of humor. Sometimes it was better to get upset and show it. And it struck Abby that it must get pretty lonely if you always tried to be funny.

"Hey, there are hot fudge sundaes for dessert," Abby finally said, and Roberta managed to arrange her face into a smile. "We can't blow our one chance to get a decent meal out of this place." Roberta dutifully trotted after her back to the picnic.

By afternoon Roberta seemed cheerier and the rest of the day whizzed by so fast it seemed to Abby like a movie speeded up with everyone racing around crazily from one activity to another. First there was a mother-daughter softball game which, despite two homers from Bonnie, was won by the mothers 7-4. Then there was a free swim with the parents allowed in, too, and for almost an hour Abby forced Daddy to play dolphin rides, letting them straddle his back while he swam underwater.

"This is the life," Daddy sighed, floating on his back. "Don't let me ever hear you complaining about this place."

Abby looked at Roberta and they rolled their eyes.

When it came to camp, Daddy had a lot to learn.

After swimming Abby assembled with the rest of the camp in the playhouse where they serenaded the parents. Between songs Abby could hear a refrain of sniffling and noses being blown. In a few minutes the serenade would be over and so would Parents' Visiting Day.

"It's certainly been a wonderful day," Aunt Tillie stood up after the last song and faced the audience. "But now I want everyone to say goodbye *right here*." The parents listened solemnly, like a group of obedient campers themselves. "*No* campers are to go out on the flagpole field. There are too many cars parked there and I don't want *any* accidents."

Outside Abby found her parents who hugged Roberta and told her they hoped to see her in New York.

"It's so typical of this place," Abby said angrily as she clung to Ma and Daddy. "Here they go and wait until everybody's stopped being homesick, *then* they have the parents come up. So now everyone can start being homesick all over again." Abby felt her mouth, nose, and eyes get all set to cry, but then she caught a sideways glimpse of Roberta, and immediately she stopped.

A minute later Ma and Daddy were heading for their car while Abby walked in silence to the Mess Hall with Roberta. They passed Gwendolyn from Pansy who was flanked on either side by her parents. Weird, thought Abby, who figured Gwendolyn of anybody would be near hysterics about now. Instead, she was all smiles.

Then during dinner Abby looked over and noticed a

glaringly empty spot at the Pansy table. Suddenly the two events clicked together like magnets. "Gwendolyn from Pansy left!" Abby announced in an astonished voice to no one in particular. She was surprised to feel more contempt than envy. Abby remembered the night her parents had called her at the infirmary and how she would have given *any*thing then for them to take her home. Now that seemed like ages ago, and yet, Abby realized, it was only about three weeks. Funny how things changed. Funny how she had managed to stick it out. She had to admit it gave her an odd sense of accomplishment.

That night before bed, everyone was unusually quiet. Abby looked at her mattress, still rumpled and sunk in from when Daddy had taken a nap during rest hour, and felt a wave of homesickness.

"Just remember. I don't want anybody getting sick on candy," Marty warned before she switched off the lights. She was wearing a new blue windbreaker which Abby guessed was the present from Lisa's parents. Everyone looked at her with expressions of blank innocence. "Oh, I know you've got it, and personally I couldn't care less how much you stuff yourselves. But nobody better wake up in the middle of the night and expect *me* to take them to the infirmary."

As soon as Marty left, the rustling of many paper bags could be heard, and, in a burst of communal feeling, everyone decided to pool their resources. Abby chomped away on peanut brittle, tore off long shoestrings of red licorice; gobbled down half-melted chocolate kisses and sucked red hot fireballs until her mouth was numb. Soon she began to feel a little better. *"Buenas noches,"* she whispered to Roberta and Eileen as she crawled under the covers. Whew! What a long day it had been. She played with the locket around her neck, and suddenly, the vision of a new, changed Merle made all the candy do a little dance inside her. Abby squeezed her eyes shut to block out the scary image. No use thinking about that now when there wasn't anything she could do. Abby sighed, turned over, and plumped her pillow into a nice, comforting shape. Then, just before she fell asleep, she spotted the flowered egg. It was perched on her window sill. Roberta had her glasses off, so Abby knew she wouldn't see when she quickly reached out and shoved the egg into an empty pocket of her shoe bag. Somehow, looking at that cheerful egg made her saddest of all.

12

July 31

Dear Ma and Daddy,

By some miracle our bunk got perfect marks in inspection for a whole week so yesterday Aunt Tillie drove us into town to Sparky's Ice Cream Parlor. It was great. We could order whatever we wanted. I got a button that said "I Finished the Pig's Special at Sparky's." Aunt Tillie put away a whole banana split. She's not so bad after all!

Everything's fine except I'm really scared about my diving test. It's the only one I have left for dolphin. I'll never be able to do it. Never. Do you think you could please call Aunt Tillie with an excuse? Make up anything you want. Maybe you could say Dr. Prince just found out I have a fractured skull or water on the brain or something, and that I shouldn't dive under any condition. Please do it right away.

Love,
Abby

Abby was nervously chewing on the strap of her bathing cap. She stood at the end of the long line in Laurel's diving class. There was a sour taste in her mouth that made her feel like she could throw up any minute. "Gee, Ma. Thanks a bunch," Abby grumbled to herself. "Where are you when I need you?" With growing dread she watched the procession in front of her. Boing!

off the board. Splash! into the water. One by one each girl plunged while Laurel, her sailor cap pulled way down against the sun, shouted encouraging suggestions.

In went Bonnie, legs flailing wildly.

"Try and keep those ankles *locked* together," Laurel called out. Then Abby felt her knees collapse as Laurel focused a reassuring smile her way. "Abby, there's absolutely nothing to be nervous about. Just remember, the trick is to keep your head tucked down and the rest of your body will automatically follow." Laurel put down her clipboard and demonstrated on dry land. "Really. You're going to do fine."

Sure, sure, thought Abby. They probably said the same thing to Custer. She stepped onto the edge of the board. It was like walking the plank.

"Just keep your head down." Laurel sounded so calm and reassuring. Then suddenly her voice jumped an octave. "Abby, I said KEEP YOUR—"

THWACK! Abby's entire body felt like it had been smacked with a wet sheet. Abby tried crying out, but all the wind was knocked out of her. She seemed to be sinking down, down in the water and for one horrible second she didn't think she'd surface.

"Don't panic. Just relax." Laurel was suddenly beside her in the water. She swung an arm around Abby's middle. Then Abby felt herself being dredged up onto the dock where the class hovered around her.

"You're okay. Just let yourself catch your breath," Laurel said, kneeling beside her.

"Geez, what a belly flop!" Bonnie said.

"Wow, look at her face—how red it is," said another voice.

"See. I *told* you!" Abby finally gasped. "I *knew* that was going to happen." She glared at Laurel who looked funny now without her sailor cap. Her wet blond hair was sticking out in all directions.

"Abby, now calm down. You were *positive* you were going to hurt yourself. So you did."

"Thank you, Dr. Freud," Abby snapped, sitting up and yanking off her cap. "You must think I'm some kind of masochist."

"What I think is that you should try another dive right away," Laurel said evenly. "That's what you do if you fall off a horse—get right back on again."

Abby managed to get up and find her sweatshirt. "I don't ride and I have absolutely no intention of going near that diving board again."

"Oh no?" Laurel's voice was stubborn. "Let's get one thing straight. As long as you're in my class, I mean to see that you dive."

But by the end of the week, Abby still hadn't gone in head first.

Come on, kid. You can do it—everyone else is, Abby would say to psych herself up. Then she'd stare down at the water. It looked so far below. Blood would begin to thrum in her head; her knees turned watery and—KERPLASH!—in she jumped.

"Here she comes, ladies and gentlemen," Bonnie would shout. "Abby Kimmel! About to try another death-defying *jump!*"

89

Abby didn't even give Bonnie a withering look. She felt too humiliated. She didn't even blame Bonnie for making fun. If only Ma would write an excuse and get her out of this mess.

August 4
Dear Ma,
Please! *Write or call Aunt Tillie and get me out of diving. I can't do it. I just can't. Make up any excuse you want.*
Desperately yours,
Abby

August 5
Dear Ma,
This is the last time I'm asking. *Please.* *I'll never ask you for another favor again. I swear.*
Your devoted daughter,
Abby

Ma just *had* to come through for her. Abby was even having nightmares about diving. A couple of nights later she dreamt she was in the circus. "The amazing Abby," the ringmaster shouted while she climbed up, up an incredibly high ladder to a long and narrow diving board. Far below was a pool of water that looked no bigger than a thimble. In the audience Ma, Daddy, Emily, Roberta, and Merle were all staring up at her expectantly.

Abby tried shouting there was some mistake, but someone was poking her in the back, pushing her forward. . . .

She jerked awake. Someone *was* poking her. It was Roberta.

"You were talking in your sleep," she whispered. "It sounded interesting."

"I was having a nightmare. . . . a real whopper." Abby sat up, her heart still thumping. "Thanks for waking me."

Roberta crept back to bed.

"Listen," Abby said. "Let's go tonight!"

"Sure. Only how about telling me *where?*"

"The counselors' shack, dummy. We keep talking about it, but if we don't go soon, the summer will be over."

"I can't see," Roberta whispered. "Is Marty here?"

"No. Her bed's empty. She's probably still at the shack."

"Then what are we waiting for?" Roberta fumbled for her glasses; Abby remembered the flashlight. They grabbed their robes and opened the screen door . . . very . . . carefully.

Abby shivered from a delicious sense of danger. "The coast is clear!" she said and then giggled. "You know, I've always wanted a chance to say that."

Soon they reached the lake; off to the right was the woods where they followed a path cleared by the thousands of counselor feet that had made the trip before them. The thick pine trees completely blocked out the moon and made the night seem doubly dark and spooky. Abby shivered again. She had the distinct feeling that any moment a counselor might creep up and grab them from behind. She clasped Roberta's hand and carefully they picked their way over tree roots and rocks until finally the woods thinned and they could make out light from the windows of the counselors' shack.

Roberta started to run. Abby held her back. "We better crawl the rest of the way."

"*Crawl!* Are you for real?"

"You don't want us to get caught, do you? And this way it'll be like in a war movie. You know. Crossing into enemy territory."

Roberta shrugged and dropped to the ground beside Abby. Finally they scrambled under a back window and peeked inside the cabin. Marty, Josie, and two other counselors were sitting around a rickety table playing cards; another counselor stood by a mirror curling her hair; and Laurel was sprawled in an old armchair reading a magazine.

"This is *it?*" Abby whispered incredulously. "Gee, it's not exactly Sin City. Maybe we came on a bad night."

"Nah, we should have known." Roberta sounded disgusted. "The counselors are too dippy to have any place good—hey, look at that! They're eating the brownies my housekeeper sent up! I recognize the tin."

"Dummy, what'd you think? That they throw out all the stuff that's sent to us? Shhh now." Abby could hear Marty.

"Time to grab a little gusto, you guys?" she was saying.

"That's from a commercial," Abby whispered. "It means they're gonna drink beer."

Roberta twirled her finger. "Whoop-ee!"

"At least they're doing *something* that's against the rules."

Abby watched Marty go over to the far corner of the room where she dramatically produced two six-packs from a plastic bag.

"Frosty cold and dee-licious," she said, tossing a can to each counselor.

Laurel took a long sip. "That sure tastes good."

"You're really incredible, Marty," said another counselor. "Not just hiding the beer, but keeping it so cold. How *do* you do it?"

"That's my little secret."

"Oh, go on and tell them, Marty," Josie said.

"Weeelll . . . all right. It's simple. I hid them in the water cooler by Sunflower. There's another six-pack there right now."

The counselors all had a good laugh over that.

"Weird." Abby ducked down, giggling. "They sound like they actually *like* Marty. Hey, we better go. We don't want to press our luck, and anyway I just thought of a great idea." She whispered it to Roberta.

"Say, that's not bad!"

A few minutes later they emerged from the woods by the lake. They made one small stop, then sneaked back to the porch of Buttercup where, from their bathrobe pockets, they each produced a can of beer. "Frosty cold and dee-licious." Abby giggled.

"I still say we should have stolen the whole six-pack."

"That's 'cause you're a pig."

They popped off the tops and clinked cans.

"*L'chaim!*" said Abby, which was what Grandma always said for a toast.

"Barf city!" Roberta shuddered. "This stuff's disgusting."

Abby took another sip and squinched her eyes. "Gross, but we should finish them just on principle."

"Yeah, and on principle I'll probably puke all over you."

They poured out the rest and left the empty cans on the top porch step.

"Marty'll be sure to spot them there," Roberta said with satisfaction before they crept into the bunk.

"How dry I am," Abby sang softly, tripping as she got into bed. She giggled. "I think maybe I *am* drunk."

"Not drunk, just spastic."

"Look who's talking!"

"Good night," Roberta whispered.

"Good night," Abby snuggled under the covers. Maybe the counselors' shack hadn't been all it was cracked up to be. Still, she felt she'd grabbed quite a bit of gusto for one night.

"She sure looks nervous," Abby observed happily the next morning. During breakfast Marty turned to Josie at the table behind her and hissed, "If that's your idea of a joke, I don't think it's very funny."

Roberta nudged Abby who choked on her milk so that it went up her nose and sprayed all over the table.

"Brother! What a bunch of pigs," snapped Marty. She shoved some napkins at Abby. "Quit that stupid giggling and mop up the mess."

"Why don't you let us all in on what's so funny," Lisa said. "It's not very nice to have private jokes."

"Oh, there's no joke," Abby said, breaking up again.

"Will you cool it!" Roberta muttered. "Marty's gonna get suspicious."

"Sorry. I'm just in such a good mood."

"Make that *great* mood," Abby said when they got back to the bunk for cleanup, for there on her bed was a special delivery letter.

Abby, Ma's neat round writing said, *I am sick to death of hearing about diving. I certainly won't make up any crazy excuses for you, but I am mailing another special delivery letter to Aunt Tillie explaining the situation. I hope you are satisfied.*

Satisfied? thought Abby. Was she ever! "My worries are over," she shouted, tossing the letter in the air.

At lunch, the camp secretary came over to the Buttercup table and told Abby that Aunt Tillie wanted to see her in the office.

Abby chewed her lip nervously. "She's probably going to try to get me to change my mind," she said to Roberta. "But fat chance!" Abby pulled out her chair and, steeling herself for the encounter, marched into the small office off the kitchen where she found Aunt Tillie sitting behind a large metal desk, checking over mimeographed schedules. She paid no attention to Abby who stood staring uncomfortably at a wall calendar from Herbert's Butcher Shop. There was a picture of a smiling cow and below it said, "When it comes to meat, we can't be beat."

Finally Aunt Tillie looked up. The look of disapproval—or was it disappointment?—on her face made

Abby swallow hard.

"Abby, I received your mother's letter. I've explained everything to Laurel so she won't be expecting you in her diving class from now on."

Abby shifted her weight nervously and murmured thank you.

"There's no reason to thank me—I can tell you that right now." She tapped the schedules into a neat pile. "I've also told Karen that you will be helping her out with the guppies for the rest of the summer."

Abby's mouth fell open. Wow! Spending every swim period with Roberta and Eileen! "You mean it?"

"Of course I mean it. Laurel tells me you're a fine swimmer and I have no intention of seeing that go to waste. And I also don't mind telling you, Abby, it bothers me to see anybody give up on getting something they want." Aunt Tillie's sharp eyes took in Abby closely. "You did want to become a dolphin, didn't you?"

Abby felt her cheeks burn. Aunt Tillie was being unfair. It wasn't as if she hadn't tried. "You don't understand—"

"I think I do. Now run along," Aunt Tillie said flatly.

During swim period Abby swam back and forth across the Fish Bowl, demonstrating the crawl and trying to forget the look on Aunt Tillie's face. She was just trying to make me feel guilty, Abby told herself. Well, it wasn't going to work. Period.

"Class, I hope you were watching closely," Karen the guppy swim counselor said when Abby had finished two laps.

"Yes, Karen," the guppies answered in a chorus. They were spread out on the dock flat on their stomachs, kicking rhythmically and moving their arms.

"Very good. Now we'll try it for real."

There was a small tidal wave as all the guppies jumped in the water to swim. "Eileen," Abby said patiently, "you have to use your arms and legs *both at the same time*."

"I know, I know," glubbed Eileen, slowly sinking.

"I just don't understand it," Roberta spluttered next to her. "I swim so *beautifully* on land."

Abby spent all of that week's swim periods holding onto the guppies while they flailed and kicked and struggled just to stay afloat. It was tiring work. And hazardous, too. Roberta kicked her in the mouth by accident and Eileen clung to her so tightly Abby was afraid they'd both drown.

"You happen to be an excellent teacher," Karen told her after a swim period. "Some of the girls are starting to make real progress."

Abby smiled. "I never taught anybody anything before—it's fun." Then without meaning to, she caught herself staring over at the diving area. Laurel's probably really sore, Abby figured. Or maybe she's *glad* to have me out of the class. She watched Bonnie finish a dive, the best one she'd ever done. Laurel was patting her on the back.

At dinner that night Bonnie announced, "Laurel says I have a good chance of passing. What happens a lot, she says, is that you don't seem to be getting anywhere and all of a sudden it just clicks." Bonnie looked pointedly at Abby. "It looks like I'll be the first—and

97

only—dolphin in our group."

"Rooty toot toot," Abby said, shoving in another forkful of mystery meat.

The next day Roberta swam, all by herself, halfway across the Fish Bowl.

"I knew you could do it!" Abby screamed from the dock, holding up her fingers in a victory sign.

Roberta beamed and gasped. "I feel like I just swam the English Channel."

"Didn't I keep telling you to keep the faith? I knew you could do it!" Suddenly her own words made Abby feel very uneasy.

Later, as she was leaving the waterfront, Laurel stopped her. "Can I speak to you for a sec?" she said.

"Sure, if you want," Abby avoided Laurel's eyes. "I was scared maybe you weren't talking to me after—well, you know."

"Granted you were being a royal pain in the rear, but I've been thinking it over and I was being pretty stubborn too. I just thought if I got tough, you'd dive and . . . well, I just hope you didn't quit the class because of me."

"It wasn't 'cause of you, Laurel. Honest." Abby pulled on the strap of her cap. "I was just too chicken."

Laurel smiled warmly. "I wish you'd come back and give it one more try—it'd make me feel a lot better."

"I'll think about it. Really I will." But as Abby walked away she realized she had already made up her mind.

Right before dinner she knocked faintly at the door of Aunt Tillie's office.

"Come in."

Do it and do it *fast,* Abby ordered herself. She fixed her eyes on the friendly cow from Herbert's Butcher Shop. "Uh—I've thought it over, and if it's okay, I'd like to go back in Laurel's diving class tomorrow."

Aunt Tillie didn't say anything. She had her hands folded together on the desk and she seemed to be thinking about something very hard.

"That was all I came to ask," Abby said meekly.

"In that case, I'll tell Laurel to be expecting you." Aunt Tillie stood up and placed a firm hand on Abby's shoulder. "Oh, and Abby. One more thing."

Abby looked at her questioningly.

"Good luck!"

"Today is your lucky day!" Roberta pranced around Abby as she and Eileen escorted her down to the lake. "I feel it in my bones."

Abby looked at them doubtfully. "I think eating those scrambled eggs at breakfast was a BIG mistake. I'm scared I'm going to puke." Abby nervously rubbed one of the rabbits' feet in her sweatshirt pocket. "It was really sweet of you guys to give me all this good luck stuff."

"I'm not sure about the shrunken head," Eileen said in a worried voice, "whether it's for good luck or not."

Abby managed to smile her appreciation and when they reached the waterfront, she squeezed their hands. "This is where we part company," she gulped out, but instead of joining the other guppies by the Fish Bowl, Roberta continued toward the diving area. "Sur-prise!"

she trilled. "I asked Karen and she said it's okay for me to come with you to diving."

Abby stopped dead on the dock. "Like fun you are!" That was all she needed. An audience!

"Don't be stupid." A stubborn look came into Roberta's eyes. "I'll give you moral support."

"You'll only make me more nervous," Abby insisted. She wagged an accusatory finger. "I *know* you, Roberta. You won't just sit. You'll start winking and holding up crossed fingers and—"

"I will do nothing of the kind." Roberta sounded insulted. "And if I want to watch Laurel's diving class, I have a perfect right."

Abby clamped her hands on her hips and shot daggers at Roberta. "Well, thanks a heap!" Then she stalked off to the diving area with Roberta tagging maddeningly behind.

August 15
Dear Ma and Daddy,

Guess what? You'll never guess!

I dived (dove? who cares!) All I know is I did it!

For almost the whole period I was jumping in, just like always. Then one time I was standing on the end of the board, trying really hard to get up the guts to dive. Roberta kept yelling good luck and telling me how I shouldn't be scared. I turned around to tell her to shut up. That's when I lost my balance. All I remember is crouching my head down cause I was afraid I was going to hurt myself.

The next thing, Roberta is jumping up and down on the dock and Laurel is giving me the V for victory sign. It was all an accident! But once I did one dive, I could do it again and

again. Now I could kill myself for all those days I missed. Keep your fingers crossed that I pass.

Last night we had Dagwood Night. Three picnic tables full of salami and cheese and stuff were set up on the flagpole field. Everybody gets two pieces of bread and you make as big a sandwich as you want. A girl in Bluebell made one that was seven inches high—someone measured it. She ate it all but threw up and had to go to the infirmary.

Roberta took this picture of me with my sandwich. I won't tell you what's in it because you might throw up too!

Love,

Abby

P.S. By accident, Roberta blew a piece of bubble gum in my hair. Marty finally had to cut it out so don't get upset when you see me. The left side of my head kind of has a bald spot.

13

IT WAS rest period. Bonnie and Phyllis were playing jacks. Everybody else was reading quietly except Abby who lay on her bed studying the familiar yellow stationery that said "A Message from Merle" on the top.

Although she'd read the letter twice now, Abby still wasn't sure what about it disturbed her. Merle had apologized over and over for not writing, saying she didn't blame Abby if she was ready to kill her. It was just that she had been so busy, Merle had explained, painting scenery, handing out programs, even having a walk-on part in a play called *Our Town*.

Some excuse, Abby snorted to herself. I haven't exactly been twiddling my thumbs, she thought, but I managed to write.

But what bothered her even more was that Merle barely mentioned her friend Nancy. All she said was how "she turned out not to be such a bad kid after all" and Merle didn't say one word about having her ears pierced.

It was as if Merle was keeping stuff from her deliberately, but why?

Abby glanced at Roberta who was engrossed in a Judy Blume book that she held about an inch from her nearsighted eyes. Roberta and Merle. It was hard to think of two more different people.

Abby played nervously with Merle's locket while she brooded over the problem at hand—how to answer Merle's letter. Should she come right out and tell her all the stuff that was worrying her? But how could you ask someone if she was still your best friend? No. That would sound too weird and babyish. Abby sighed and, fishing out her letter box from underneath her bed, figured she'd just have to wait until she got home to see what was up with Merle.

August 16
Dear Merle,

Thanks for finally writing. You're right. I was ready to kill you but I guess I can find it in my kind, wonderful heart to forgive you.

All that stuff you're doing at the theater sounds neat. Our bunk is finally getting to do a play. Well, it's not a play exactly, but sort of a skit. Each summer there are two birthday parties for the whole camp, one in July for all the kids born between January and June and another one in August for the rest of the year. The skit is supposed to have something to do with birthdays or the months of the year. In the July skit each girl was a holiday. Like February was a Valentine. I hope we come up with something better than that.

Last night Aunt Tillie had our group up to her house to watch some dumb Disney movie. It was the first time I had seen TV in weeks! Will I have a lot of catching up to do. Grandma has been filling me in on "Live for Today." Did you know that Owen and Tiffany got married?

That's all for now. I won't even bother to say "Write" but you better!!!

> *Yours till Niagara Falls,*
> *Abby*

P.S. I almost forgot to tell you—I finally learned to dive so I may even get to be a dolphin. Bonnie just passed, the lucky dog. We all had to sing "Congratulations to You" at dinner. I just mouthed the words.

"So? Who's going to come up with an idea?" Marty was stretched out on one of the wood benches, pockmarked with campers' names and initials, that lined the Pinecrest playhouse. Outside, rain beat down steadily, thrumming against the windows. "You've got only four days. Not that I care, but personally I think you're all going to look pretty stupid standing up on stage with no skit. So how's about it? Abby?"

"Wha-?" mumbled Abby. She was engrossed in a book called *Your Favorite Movie Monsters* which a girl in Bluebell had traded her for two "Tales of Horror" comic books.

"Abby, if it's not asking too much, would you stop reading and pay attention?"

"Sorry." Abby stuck her finger in the book to keep her place. "No, I don't have any ideas."

"And if I did," Abby whispered to Roberta, "it would be on how to get this stupid rain to stop!" Abby glared outside. "If this keeps up, I'll never pass my dives and goodbye dolphin."

"It'll stop."

"That's what you said yesterday."

"What if we were flowers," Lisa was saying. "Like we could each be the flower for a different month and recite a poem." She snapped her fingers as if the most brilliant idea had just hit her. "I know! We could call it 'The Birthday Bouquet!'"

"ARRRGGGH!" Bonnie clutched her throat.

"Excuse me while I go barf," Roberta said.

"Aunt Tillie named the bunks after flowers," Lisa said defensively. "I bet *she'd* like it."

"It still stinks," Phyllis said flatly. "What about doing the signs of the zodiac?"

"Dummy," Roberta told her. "They did that last year. Come on, Abby. Don't you have even *one* idea?"

"If she does," Bonnie tapped her head, "it'll die of loneliness."

"Lookit, Einstein," Abby snapped. "I don't see you coming up with any brainstorms." Then suddenly her eye happened to catch a page in her book. "Maybe I *do* have an idea," Abby said slowly. "What about doing something with monsters?"

"How appropriate," muttered Marty.

"Yuck, yuck," Abby said sourly. She continued with growing enthusiasm. "What we could do is have it be one of the monster's birthdays and all the other monsters like Dracula and the Mummy and Mr. Hyde could be the guests."

"It's better than flowers," Phyllis admitted.

"At the cookout before, maybe everybody could come in costume, like at a Halloween party," Eileen suggested.

"I still like my idea," insisted Lisa, looking toward Marty for approval.

"Tough. Nobody else does," Roberta said. "And I know that you of all people—being prize camper and everything—wouldn't want to be a *bad* sport about this. Right?''

Lisa shut up.

''Well then,'' Roberta said. ''That makes it unanimous.''

''It should be Dracula's birthday because Abby does a real good Bela Lugosi,'' Eileen said with a nod.

Bonnie smugly folded her arms. ''Now we know the real reason she suggested this.''

Abby jumped up in protest. ''For your information, I don't want the lead,'' she said hotly. It was one thing to fool around in front of your friends. But perform in front of the whole camp? All those eyes watching you! No way, thought Abby.

''Come off it,'' Roberta said. ''You do that vampire routine great.'' She pushed Abby in front of the group. ''Now shut up and do your stuff.''

Abby eyed her audience apprehensively. The biggest part in her whole life had been head rat in a second grade production of *The Pied Piper*. And all that had involved was a lot of squeaking. But now she had a chance to be the star. *Star*. The very word thrilled her and, with a shrug, Abby began rolling her eyes and smiling fiendishly. ''Vell, since you are tvisting my arm. . . .'' Then she held up a warning hand. ''But no applause, please!''

August 17
Dear Ma and Daddy,
Fame at last! I'm the star of our skit. I get to play Dracula. I just pray I don't goof up all my lines. I'm so nervous. At

school I'm always stuck in the chorus. I never had to worry about stuff like this before.

By the way, I can't find one of my fang teeth so could you send me another pair special delivery (they always have them at Buddy's Toyland on Broadway). Thanks a lot.

Love,
Me

The next morning, when they had all reassembled in the playhouse, Marty ran down the cast. "Abby, you're all set as Dracula; Bonnie's Frankenstein—"

"Talk about typecasting!" Abby couldn't resist.

"That's enough of that! Phyllis, you're playing Mr. Hyde. Roberta's the Mummy. Eileen is—?"

"King Kong," chirped Eileen who loved monkeys almost as much as gerbils and dogs.

Marty frowned. "Well, that leaves just you, Lisa."

"What about the Hunchback of Notre Dame?" Bonnie suggested.

"Well . . all right," Lisa agreed unenthusiastically.

"Or the Bride of Frankenstein?" Abby said. "That'd be kind of funny. Having a Mr. and Mrs."

"Whatever you guys want," Lisa said. "I'm perfectly willing to go along with whatever the group wants."

Roberta snorted. "How noble!"

"I have an idea," Eileen said with a sheepish smile. "It's a little corny maybe, but it would sort of give the skit a twist at the end. What about this?" Then she shyly outlined her plot idea.

"Corny isn't the word!" Bonnie said when Eileen finished.

"I like it!" Lisa announced.

"Settled, then," said Roberta. "And now we better get cracking on costumes and rehearsing."

"Forget about finding anything in here," Abby said, rummaging through the costume closet backstage. It was filled with old ballgowns, kimonos, cowboy hats, and a dusty pink feather boa which Abby flung around her neck dramatically.

"We better go around to all the bunks," Roberta suggested, "and see what we can turn up."

In slickers and rainboots, everybody dashed outside. An hour later they came dripping back into the playhouse.

"I got these," Phyllis held up a pair of furry mittens and a fright wig, "for when I change from Dr. Jekyll into Mr. Hyde."

Roberta had found two torn sheets to rip into bandages for the Mummy; Eileen had borrowed a rubbery gorilla mask from a girl in Marigold. "And a counselor's loaning me a black cape," Abby said excitedly. "It's perfect. When I make my grand entrance, I can sort of swoop around the audience, unfurling it."

"Get her," said Roberta. "Yesterday, you couldn't get her up on stage. Today she's turning it into a one-woman show!"

The morning of the birthday party, the whole camp trooped into breakfast to find an invitation on every table.

Tonight you are cordially invited to a

MONSTROUS FEAST

of

Frankfurters à la Frankenstein

Draculaburgers

King Kong Kola
and, for dessert,

Mummified Marshmallows

Come in Costume

Following the cookout will be a
celebration of

Dracula's Birthday

BE THERE . . . . . OR ELSE!

By dinnertime the rain finally stopped but the ground was still so soggy that every poncho in the camp had to be spread on the flagpole field for the cookout. Four fires crackled away and grew brighter and brighter as evening fell. Abby was polishing off her sixth toasted marshmallow, licking the last of the lovely goo off her fingers, when Marty began rounding up everybody from Buttercup and herding them into the playhouse.

A few minutes later Abby stood mesmerized in front of the large mirror backstage. Her face was now powdered to a chalky white with heavy black penciled eyebrows and cruel red lips. She enfolded her cape around her, arched an eyebrow, and bared her fang teeth ever so slightly.

"Abby, you can stop admiring yourself," Marty said. "Aunt Tillie just came in and it looks like almost everybody's seated." She looked at the girls around her. "I guess it's curtain time."

Abby squeezed a bandaged hand that belonged to the mummified Roberta. Only the glint of her glasses gave any hint of her identity. "No offense," Abby giggled. "But you look like an accident waiting for someplace to happen."

"Very funny," came Roberta's muffled voice from under her wrappings.

"Wish me luck!" Abby said. "I'm so nervous, I could pee." Then she ducked out the backstage exit and sneaked around to the porch where she watched the curtain go up and waited for her entrance cue.

So far, so good, Abby thought as the skit unfolded. No lines forgotten and the audience was laughing in all the right places. Even Eileen was really hamming it up, beating her chest, making apelike grunts, and kissing a doll that was supposed to be the beautiful girl King Kong had captured.

"This better be the last birthday for Dracula we ever have to come to," intoned Bonnie in the slow, menacing voice of Frankenstein. "I'm sick of his bossing us around. He treats us like slaves."

"You have my word. Tonight we will finally have our revenge on the old bloodsucker," cackled Phyllis/Mr. Hyde, casting a meaningful glance at a large wrapped package on stage. "Just wait until he opens his surprise!"

Almost time! Now I come in and go up on the stage from the left, Abby told herself calmly. Or was it *stage* left? Which would really mean from the right. Which was it? Cold sweat trickled under Abby's arms. Oh God!—

Mr. Hyde cackled again and pointed a hairy paw at the door to the playhouse. "SHHHH!" I hear him coming now."

Then all heads in the theater turned as the door flung open. "Gud ee-ven-ing!" Abby managed to creak out with a flourish of her cape. "Ze birthday boy is here!"

Her tongue felt thick and furry yet somehow the words floated out all by themselves. Abby began weaving in and out of the aisles toward the stage, furling and unfurling her cape, and her numbness began to subside. She paused dramatically in front of Laurel. "Duhn't you vant to vish me a happy birthday, my dolling?" she said, chucking her under the chin.

The audience laughed loudly.

"We have been expecting you," said Phyllis which Abby knew was her cue to go on stage. Instead she found herself circling through the audience once more, sweeping over to a girl still in a devil costume. "Vat a looovely outfit," she crooned. "Red has alvays been my favorite color."

More laughter and suddenly Abby stopped short in front of Aunt Tillie. "My, but duhn't you look like a juicy vun!" she cried with a fiery look in her eyes. The audience went wild; Aunt Tillie laughed too.

"WE HAVE BEEN EXPECTING YOU," Phyllis repeated with an edge to her voice.

Rats! thought Abby. Just when I'm really starting to roll. Reluctantly she took her place onstage.

"Cheers!" Abby raised a glass of tomato juice and drank it down. "Mmmm. Type B-negative. Soooo tasty!"

Then the the monsters sang to the slow strains of "Yo! Heave Ho!"

Hap-pee Birth-*day*
Hap-pee Birth-*day*
There is sadness in the air
Gloom and doom are everywhere
Hap-pee Birth-*day*

Abby pointed in surprise to the big present on stage. "Vat? A present for ME! But you shouldn't have." And she rushed to unwrap it. "I vonder what it could be." Abby yanked off the bow which released the sides of the package and suddenly there stood . . . Super-camper!

"Dracula, you have met your match," cried Lisa, dressed in a Pinecrest T-shirt and shorts and a towel cape emblazoned with "Supercamper." Chasing Abby around the stage, she vowed to take the other monsters away from the Count's castle for a fun-filled summer at Pinecrest.

"Ve vill see about dat," said Abby, baring her fangs.

Then Supercamper produced a long string of garlic. Brandishing it in front of Abby's face, she explained for those in the audience who'd never seen a vampire movie that it would render Dracula harmless. "You are power-less now!" she cried. "Oh fiend of the night."

"Not dat—anything but dat!" Hissing, Abby shrank from the garlic, covering her face with her cape, and backed offstage where Marty quickly attached a wired belt to her waist.

"Dracula begone," commanded Supercamper, wav-ing the garlic again.

Abby swooped back on stage and bared her fangs one final time. "I vill be back!" Then Marty gave a tug on the wires which were connected to a pulley from the rafters and off she flew, flapping her cape like bat wings.

Everybody gasped at the showstopper and the skit ended, the audience clapping enthusiastically as the girls in Buttercup took their bows. Offstage, Marty tried to disentangle Abby from the wired belt. "Hold still!" she said impatiently. "Your fans will wait." Then Abby

rushed out to join the cast and suddenly the applause grew distinctly louder. For me, she realized. For *me*.

Abby tried smiling modestly around her fang teeth.

"A star is born," said Roberta beside her.

"You were terrific," Eileen whispered.

I really was, thought Abby. And then the curtain came down.

August 21
Dear Merle,

I can't wait to see you. It won't be long now. Three days and I'm home! I wish you were going to be there but Labor Day isn't so far off. What movies do you want to see? I'm dying to see the one about giant cockroaches invading New York.

Last night was our skit. I played Dracula which maybe sounds dumb to you after all the real shows you've seen this summer. Afterwards we had a party at Aunt Tillie's. Bonnie left in the middle with Marty because she got her period for the first time. She won't talk about it to anyone. Not even Phyllis. I remember when my cousin Shelley got it, she announced it to the entire world, but she was almost 14. I guess it's different if you're not even 11 yet. I feel kind of bad for her, being the only one.

Well, that's all for now. See you real soon.

    Yours till Bear Mountain has cubs,
     Abby

P.S. I almost forgot. I'm bringing home two of the mice. Bambi for me and the one I wrote about—Fred Astaire—for you. Eileen is also taking one and the other two are going with Maya, the nature counselor.

August 22
Dear Ma and Daddy,

    Our skit was a hit. Everybody said I was great, even Aunt Tillie. The next day some of the younger kids would scream and run away whenever they saw me. I felt like a real star.

    A lot of the kids are nervous waiting to find out about the awards which are announced at Banquet Dinner tomorrow. I'm pretty sure I won't get anything. Drama is the only one I have a chance for.

    It looks like I can also forget about being a dolphin. My dives still aren't good enough. Laurel says she wishes she could pass me anyway. I wish she could too.

    For my first meal home, could I have a garbage pizza from Mel's (except no anchovies). I can't believe it but in 54 hours I'll be home!

Love,

Me

P.S. I just this second got a letter from Merle. Now she says she's going to Connecticut to spend a week with that kid she met. She won't be home until September 6th. Some best friend. If it was me, I'd come straight home to see her. I was going to bring home a mouse for me and a mouse for her. Now maybe I'll keep both of them.

"OUR LAST DAY. I can't believe it," Abby was saying as she finished packing. "It doesn't *feel* like the end of the summer. I mean, nothing momentous has happened."

"I survived in one piece. That's momentous enough," Roberta said, sweeping all the medicine off her shelf into a plastic zipper bag. "Last year I came home with two broken fingers."

"Ouch!" Abby cried as she fumbled with the suitcase lock. "I'm gonna break mine trying to get this stupid thing closed." Abby had stuffed in all her souvenirs of the summer—the china egg from Roberta's parents, a scrapbook of snapshots, the shrunken head from Eileen, and assorted arts and crafts projects including an elaborate Indian feather headdress for Emily. "It's lucky I couldn't find my jeans or my slicker. They wouldn't have fit in anyway." Then Abby giggled. "Somehow I have a feeling Ma isn't going to see it that way."

Late in the afternoon, everybody climbed in their bathing suits for one last swim. Abby decided not to go with the other mackerels. Instead, she jumped into the Fish Bowl with the guppies and goldfish. It wasn't just that she wanted to be with Roberta and Eileen. From the Fish Bowl, Abby couldn't see out to the dolphin float. It absolutely killed her to watch Bonnie out there.

Abby grabbed Roberta's hand. "I'm gonna show you something Laurel taught us the other day. It's called a T.B., for tushy bump, and it's really fun."

"Go find somebody else to be your guinea pig," said Roberta. She tried to paddle away but Abby's grip was firm.

"Lookit, I promise you won't drown. Just take a deep breath and when I count to three we both go underwater, understand?"

Then still holding hands, they brought their knees up close to their chests, pressed their feet against each other's . . . and pushed. Up shot their legs, their tushies bumped, and they both surfaced, spluttering and laughing.

Abby shook the water out of her eyes. *"See?* I told you it was fun."

"Eileen, come here!" Roberta was shouting. "We got something neat to show you!"

By the time the whistle for "All out" was blown, there was only an hour left until Banquet Dinner.

The girls of Buttercup busily spruced themselves up for the big night. Since Marty was nowhere in sight, everyone, except Lisa, sampled the lipsticks from her make-up case.

Abby carefully applied some "Passionately Pink." "For God's sake, don't be such a poop," she said to Lisa. "Whoever's going to be prize camper has already been picked."

"For your information, I wasn't even thinking of that," Lisa snapped.

Roberta smiled widely into the bathroom mirror and

smacked together her ruby-red lips. "This color is definitely *me!*"

"Hurry up and finish getting ready," Abby whispered to her. "Remember we have something to do before we go to the Mess Hall."

"Oh, that," Roberta said, turning down her lipsticked mouth. "I still think it's a dumb idea."

"That's your problem," Abby hissed. "You just have no sentiment. Now HURRY UP."

Abby grabbed the necessary items and pushed Roberta out the door and down to the summerhouse which was curtained off from the Mess Hall and the rest of the camp by a thick stand of birches and pine.

Abby fished out her pen and a piece of paper from her blazer pocket and carefully wrote in majestically curling letters:

By this solemn pact, we the undersigned —Abigail Frances Kimmel and Roberta Naomi Harrison — who have suffered and survived two months at Pinecrest Prison Camp are now Blood Sisters and swear loyalty to each other forever and ever.

"I'm just warning you," Roberta grumbled, "I get faint at the sight of blood—especially my own." Abby paid her no mind. She produced a safety pin from her pocket, blew the lint off it, scrinched up her eyes, and quickly jabbed her finger. A dot of red appeared. "See! That didn't hurt a bit."

"Do it and do it fast." Roberta held out her hand and turned her face away. "Ouch!"

"I haven't touched you yet!"

"OUCH! You did now." Roberta waggled her wounded hand. "I'll probably get gangrene," she grumbled. "Only for you would I do this."

Abby gazed at her fondly. "Dummy, that's the point. You're not supposed to go around jabbing yourself for just anybody."

Then they pressed their pricked fingertips together and each made a bloody fingerprint beside their signatures.

"Now it's official," Abby said with satisfaction. She knelt down and began digging up a little dirt. "This is where we'll bury our blood pact. And next year, if we're here, we can come and dig it up."

Roberta shook her head furiously. "Fat chance. There isn't going to be any next year. No way am I coming back to this dump."

"Famous last words," said Abby, leaning back on her heels. "Forget about next year. Who can tell what's going to happen then, right?" Abby had to smile at her own words. That should be my theme song, she thought.

Then they buried the letter, tamped down the ground, and placed a stone on top as a marker. "That does it," Abby said. "Now we're really blood sisters."

Roberta slung an arm around her as they headed for

the Mess Hall. "Well, I guess I was getting kind of sick of being an only child."

For Banquet Dinner the Mess Hall had been transformed with twists of green and white crepe paper looped back and forth across the ceiling and sweet-smelling pine branches on every table.

"This meal was really good," Abby paused as she worked her way through a second piece of blueberry pie and ice cream.

"They always give us a good send-off," Roberta smiled, exposing teeth stained deep purple. "I guess they figure they owe it to us before throwing us back into the cruel world, sob! sob!"

Just then Aunt Tillie stood up at the head table and like magic the room began to quiet down.

"Goody," whispered Lisa. "Now we get to the important stuff."

Bonnie looked excited too.

"The way I figure it," Phyllis told her, "you're sure to get at least five awards."

"Wow, do you think there'll be room in your house for you *and* all the trophies?" Abby asked wide-eyed.

Bonnie smiled patiently at Abby. "Jealousy is such an *ugly* emotion."

"Hey, come on, everybody," Eileen pleaded. "It's our last night."

"Thank goodness for that," muttered Marty.

First came the dubious distinction prizes. A broom was presented collectively to Larkspur for scoring the lowest marks in cleanup all summer; then a chubby girl from Phlox received the "Leadbelly" award—a bottle of Pepto-Bismol—for eating the largest sandwich at Dagwood Night. Finally Katy awarded a tongue depressor to "the infirmary's best customer—Roberta Harrison."

"Speech! Speech!" Abby shouted.

"Thank you," Roberta stood up and nodded to the crowd once the applause died down. "This is a great honor and I want you all to know I worked very hard for it. . . . Well, I guess that's all I have to say, 'cause if I talk any longer, I'll probably get laryngitis and wind up in the infirmary."

"At least one of us isn't going home empty-handed," Abby whispered, clapping her on the back.

Then Aunt Tillie rose for silence once again and began her speech. Abby gazed quite fondly at the tiny camp director who was saying how sorry she was to see the summer end. Aunt Tillie really wasn't a bad egg, Abby decided. Sure she was scary and definitely *not* the laugh riot of the century. But she was fair and she really seemed to mean all the corny stuff she said about camp.

In her clipped manner, Aunt Tillie went on about how she felt sure that for each girl, the summer had been an important one. "Now I don't like long speeches, but I do want to say that what means the most in the end is *not* how many baskets you made in arts and crafts or how many bull's-eyes you made in archery, but whether or not you have made good friends." Abby beamed at Roberta who crossed her eyes and made gagging noises. "There are some girls, however, who have shown special ability or achievement and for that they deserve recognition. So now we'll start with the presentation of awards for the different sports and activities."

"Bonnie's parents are going have to move to a bigger house to fit all her trophies," Abby whispered a while later. "She's gotten four already—archery, softball, volleyball *and* tennis," Abby counted off on her fingers. "What I don't get is how Lisa won drama. I mean, not to brag or anything, but I thought—"

"Will you shut up!" Bonnie hissed. "They're doing all the waterfront stuff now."

"That makes numero five," Abby said as Bonnie popped up to receive the boating award.

Then Laurel stood up. "For the ten year olds," she announced, "the swimming award goes to—Abby Kimmel!"

Abby clutched Roberta. "That's me! That's *me!*"

Roberta jabbed her affectionately. "Well, don't just sit here like a moron."

Abby stumbled towards Laurel who looked unfamiliar with her blond hair curled and no sun cream on the nose. "The swimming award! Me? I don't understand. I mean, it's not like I passed or anything."

"Abby, will you kindly stop yapping and take this trophy? Look, you improved and that counts too. Okay?" Laurel smiled, handing over a small brass swimmer perched on a wood base. "And from here on in, you should learn that you don't put up a fight when someone offers you a prize."

"Sorry. You know me—Miss Mouth," Abby smiled sheepishly. "And thanks."

"She didn't deserve it," Bonnie was saying when Abby returned to the table. "She only got it because they felt sorry for her."

"You can say that again," Phyllis chimed in.

"A bet's a bet," Roberta insisted. "Fork it over."

"Oh, all right." Bonnie slapped something into Roberta's outstretched hand.

"What's that all about?" asked Abby.

"Bonnie thought she was a cinch to win swimming too. But I *knew* you'd get it." Roberta looked immensely satisfied. "I was positive all along, so I bet her her last three candy bars."

"Congrats, Abby." Eileen squeezed her hand. "I'm so happy you got it."

"Hey, save the schmaltz for later, okay?" Roberta said. "They're going to announce prize campers and I got stuff riding on this too."

Lisa arranged her face into a modest smile as Aunt Tillie explained how this award was meant to honor the girl who "in countless small and often unnoticed ways has shown the most sincere spirit of kindness and helpfulness."

"And so it is with great pleasure that I present—" Lisa seemed to tense slightly in her seat—"the award for the ten year olds to Eileen Wachsman."

Eileen! Abby was stunned.

Several girls at other tables were twisting around to get a look at her.

"I don't think anyone even knows who she is," Roberta said under her breath.

"If it was up to Eileen, she'd keep it that way," Abby whispered back, thinking it was hard to tell who looked more stunned, Eileen or Lisa. "Come on, Eileen. You've got to go up and get the award."

"I hate stuff like this," Eileen wailed softly as Abby propelled her towards the head table.

Then Roberta began to reach across to Lisa who was studiously attacking another piece of pie.

"For God's sake," Abby hissed. "Can't you leave her alone?"

"She owes me two packs of gum," Roberta answered just as Eileen returned lugging an elaborate silver loving cup.

"Forget the gum, you'll live without it."

Roberta looked surprised at the tone of Abby's voice.

Lisa got up and excused herself to go to the bathroom.

"Don't tell me you feel sorry for her?" Roberta's round eyes were wide.

"Well, maybe I do . . . sort of."

Roberta snorted.

"I know she didn't deserve it. But she really wanted it. That should count for something—especially when Eileen doesn't want it at all." Abby sighed, feeling puzzled. Fair is fair, she tried telling herself, but she couldn't help feeling that fair could be unfair too.

"You're nuts," said Roberta, but when Lisa returned, she left her alone.

The awards were over now and, at Aunt Tillie's signal, everybody left the Mess Hall and began wending their way down to the lake for the last campfire. It was a beautiful night. The jet-black sky glittered with an explosion of stars and, walking among the girls in her bunk, Abby felt a curious sadness steal over her. The summer really was over. She felt it now. No more complaining about softball games she didn't want to go to, or arguing about whose turn it was to sweep the bunk, or getting yelled at by Marty or into fights with Bonnie and Phyllis. And, of course, no more Roberta. That was hardest of all to imagine. Yet, two months ago, thought Abby, being separated from Merle had seemed like the end of the world—and it hadn't been. Why was it, Abby wondered, that there was something sad realizing that too?

Abby took her place beside Roberta and Eileen in the circle around the fire by the lake. Each girl crossed her hands in front of her and took the hand of the girl standing next to her. Slowly from side to side swayed the friendship ring. The flames from the fire danced and flickered on their faces as they sang the song that had opened every campfire since the beginning of the summer. Never before had the song seemed to Abby so sweet or so sad.

Each campfire lights anew
The flame of friendship true
The joy we've had in knowing you
Will last the whole year through.

Everyone turned to her neighbor and for the last time exchanged the Pinecrest shake; then starting with the youngest girls in Sweetpea, each camper stood before Aunt Tillie, in the middle of the circle, and was handed a white candle imbedded in a small wooden boat. One by one the candles were lit and floated out onto the lake.

"You have to make a wish before you put your candle in the water,'' explained Roberta. ''Of course last year I wished I wouldn't have to come back here and you see where that got me. So much for wishes.''

Abby smiled although she couldn't help wishing Roberta would act a little more choked up about their farewell. She cupped the flame of her candle with one hand and stooped down to the water. What could she wish for, Abby wondered. That Merle would be the same old Merle when she got home? That Roberta's parents would decide to move to New York? Then suddenly Bonnie jostled her and sent her boat bobbing into the water. ''Bon-nie,'' Abby snapped. ''I wasn't ready to do mine yet.''

''Tough toenails.''

Abby watched her boat tilt and almost overturn but then it righted itself and began floating out toward the middle of the lake. So much for wishes, Abby silently repeated Roberta's words. Well, that's right, she thought. Even when they do come true, it's never exactly the way you expected anyway.

Abby stood back from the water. The tiny armada of candle boats was drifting and bobbing farther out in the lake and soon she was not sure which one was hers. The wind steered the flickering fleet onward past the dolphin raft and off toward a sandy hook of land that jutted out from the shoreline.

''I'm really going to miss you,'' Abby whispered to Roberta. She waited for a wisecrack but all Roberta said was ''Ditto.'' Then they stood watching until the last of the candles curved around the shoreline and couldn't be seen anymore.